THE DOLLY DIALOGUES

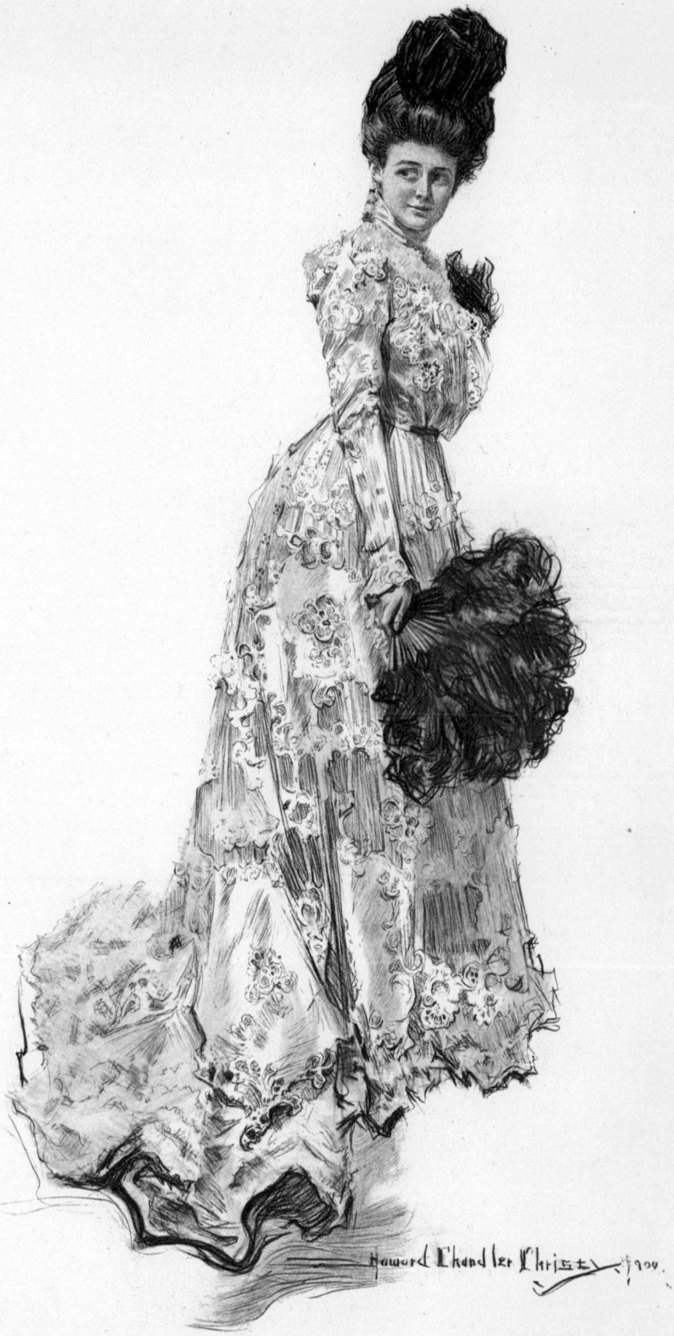
Howard Chandler Christy 1900.

The DOLLY DIALOGUES

By ANTHONY HOPE

WITH EIGHTEEN ILLUSTRATIONS BY
HOWARD CHANDLER CHRISTY

*THESE are foolish things to all the wise—
And I love wisdom more than she loves me*

NEW YORK · R. H. RUSSELL
NINETEEN HUNDRED AND ONE

COPYRIGHT 1901 BY
ROBERT HOWARD RUSSELL

UNIVERSITY PRESS . JOHN WILSON
AND SON · CAMBRIDGE, U. S. A.

CONTENTS

	PAGE
I.—A Liberal Education	9
II.—Cordial Relations	16
III.—Retribution	24
IV.—The Perverseness of It	31
V.—A Matter of Duty	39
VI.—My Last Chance	47
VII.—The Little Wretch!	55
VIII.—An Expensive Privilege	63
IX.—A Very Dull Affair	71
X.—Strange, but True	80
XI.—The Very Latest Thing	89
XII.—An Uncounted Hour	97
XIII.—A Reminiscence	105
XIV.—Ancient History	113
XV.—A Fine Day	122
XVI.—The House Opposite	129
XVII.—A Quick Change	137
XVIII.—A Slight Mistake	145

CONTENTS

	PAGE
XIX.—THE OTHER LADY	153
XX.—A LIFE SUBSCRIPTION	161
XXI.—WHAT MIGHT HAVE BEEN	169
XXII.—A FATAL OBSTACLE	178
XXIII.—THE CURATE'S BUMP	186
XXIV.—ONE WAY IN	194

List of Illustrations

Dolly	*Frontispiece*
	PAGE
Mr. Carter	10
Miss Dolly Foster	18
" Were you ever in Love ? " she asked	32
" Are n't you accustomed to your dignity yet ? " .	40
" Why, I was the man with Lady Mickleham " .	66
" There is n't," said George, " a girl in London to touch her "	84
" Lady Mickleham is usually accounted a person of considerable attractions "	92
" I 've been hearing something about you, Mr. Carter "	114
" He 's a nice boy," said she. " How like he is to you, Mr. Carter "	126
" You were sitting close by me — on a bench " .	138
" You seem very pleased with yourself," said Dolly	154
" Are n't you ever going to marry ? "	162
" Oh, mine 's a life subscription "	166
" She used to bore me awfully about you " . . .	180
" Now, is n't that provoking ? " cried Dolly. " They have n't rolled the tennis lawn " .	188
" You are an Apollo, Mr. Carter "	192

The Dolly Dialogues

I

A LIBERAL EDUCATION

"THERE'S ingratitude for you!" Miss Dolly Foster exclaimed suddenly.

"Where?" I asked, rousing myself from meditation.

She pointed at a young man who had just passed where we sat. He was dressed very smartly, and was walking with a lady attired in the height of the fashion.

"I *made* that man," said Dolly, "and now he cuts me dead before the whole of the Row! It's atrocious. Why, but for me, do you suppose he'd be at this moment engaged to three thousand a year and — and the plainest girl in London?"

"Not that," I pleaded; "think of—"

"Well, very plain, anyhow. I was quite ready to bow to him. I almost did."

"In fact, you did?"

"I did n't. I declare I did n't."

"Oh, well, you did n't, then. It only looked like it."

"I met him," said Miss Dolly, "three years ago. At that time he was — oh, quite unpresentable. He was everything he should n't be. He was a teetotaler, you know, and he did n't smoke, and he was always going to concerts. Oh, and he wore his hair long, and his trousers short, and his hat on the back of his head. And his umbrella — "

"Where did he wear that?"

"He *carried* that, Mr. Carter. Don't be silly! Carried it unrolled, you know, and generally a paper parcel in the other hand; and he had spectacles too."

"He has certainly changed outwardly at least."

"Yes, I know; well, I did that. I took him in hand, and I just taught him, and now — !"

"Yes, I know that. But how did you teach him? Give him Saturday evening lectures, or what?"

"Oh, every-evening lectures, and most-morning walks. And I taught him to dance, and I broke his wretched fiddle with my own hands!"

"What very arbitrary distinctions you draw!"

"I don't know what you mean. I do like a man to be smart, anyhow. Don't you, Mr. Carter? You're not so smart as you might be. Now, shall I take you in hand?" And she smiled upon me.

Mr. Carter

A LIBERAL EDUCATION

"Let's hear your method. What did you do to him?"

"To Phil Meadows? Oh, nothing. I just slipped in a remark here and there, whenever he talked nonsense. I used to speak just at the right time, you know."

"But how had your words such influence, Miss Foster?"

"Oh, well, you know, Mr. Carter, I made it a *condition* that he should do just what I wanted in little things like that. Did he think I was going to walk about with a man carrying a brown-paper parcel — as if we had been to the shop for a pound of tea?"

"Still, I don't see why he should alter all his — "

"Oh, you are stupid! Of course, he liked me, you know."

"Oh, did he? I see."

"You seem to think that very funny."

"Not that he did — but that, apparently, he does n't."

"Well, you got out of that rather neatly — for you. No, he does n't now. You see, he misunderstood my motive. He thought — well, I do believe he thought I cared for him, you know. Of course I did n't."

"Not a bit?"

THE DOLLY DIALOGUES

"Just as a friend — and a pupil, you know. And when he'd had his hair cut and bought a frock-coat (fancy! he'd never had one!), he looked quite nice. He has nice eyes. Did you notice them?"

"Lord, no!"

"Well, you're so unobservant."

"Oh, not always. I've observed that your—"

"Please don't! It's no use, is it?"

I looked very unhappy. There is an understanding that I am very unhappy since Miss Foster's engagement to the Earl of Mickleham was announced.

"What was I saying before — before you — you know — oh, about Phil Meadows, of course. I did like him very much, you know, or I should n't have taken all that trouble. Why, his own mother thanked me!"

"I have no more to say," said I.

"But she wrote me a horrid letter afterwards."

"You're so very elliptical."

"So very what, Mr. Carter?"

"You leave so much out, I mean. After what?"

"Why, after I sent him away. Did n't I tell you? Oh, we had the most awful scene. He *raved*, Mr. Carter. He called me the most horrid names, and—"

"Tore his hair?"

A LIBERAL EDUCATION

"It wasn't long enough to get hold of," she tittered. "But don't laugh. It was really dreadful. And so unjust! And then, next day, when I thought it was comfortably over, you know, he came back, and — and apologised, and called himself the most awful names, and — well, that was really worse."

"What did the fellow complain of?" I asked in wondering tones.

"Oh, he said I'd destroyed his faith in women, you know, and that I'd led him on, and that I was — well, he was very rude indeed. And he went on writing me letters like that for a whole year! It made me quite uncomfortable."

"But he didn't go back to short trousers and a fiddle, did he?" I asked anxiously.

"Oh, no. But he forgot all he owed me, and he told me that his heart was dead, and that he should never love any one again."

"But he's going to marry that girl."

"Oh, he doesn't care about her," said Miss Dolly, reassuringly. "It's the money, you know. He hadn't a farthing of his own. Now he'll be set up for life."

"And it's all due to you!" said I, admiringly.

"Well, it is, really."

"I don't call her such a bad-looking girl, though." (I hadn't seen her face.)

THE DOLLY DIALOGUES

"Mr. Carter! She's *hideous!*"

I dropped that subject.

"And now," said Miss Dolly again, "he cuts me dead!"

"It is the height of ingratitude. Why, to love you was a liberal education!"

"Yes, wasn't it? How nicely you put that! 'A liberal education!' I shall tell Archie." (Archie is Lord Mickleham.)

"What, about Phil Meadows?"

"Goodness me, no, Mr. Carter. Just what you said, you know."

"But why not tell Mickleham about Phil Meadows?" I urged. "It's all to your credit, you know."

"Yes, I know, but men are so foolish. You see, Archie thinks—"

"Of course he does."

"You might let me finish."

"Archie thinks you were never in love before."

"Yes, he does. Well, of course, I wasn't in love with Phil—"

"Not a little bit?"

"Oh, well—"

"Nor with any one else?"

Miss Dolly prodded the path with her parasol.

"Nor with any one else?" I asked again.

Miss Dolly looked for an instant in my direction.

A LIBERAL EDUCATION

"Nor with any one else?" said I.

Miss Dolly looked straight in front of her.

"Nor with —" I began.

"Hullo, old chappie, where did you spring from?"

"Why, Archie!" cried Miss Dolly.

"Oh, how are you, Mickleham, old man? Take this seat; I'm just off — just off. Yes, I was, upon my honour — got to meet a man at the club. Good-by, Miss Foster. Jove! I'm late!"

And as I went I heard Miss Dolly say, "I thought you were *never* coming, Archie, dear!" Well, she didn't think he was coming just then. No more did I.

II

CORDIAL RELATIONS

THE other day I paid a call on Miss Dolly Foster for the purpose of presenting to her my small offering on the occasion of her marriage to Lord Mickleham. It was a pretty little bit of jewellery,—a pearl heart, broken (rubies played the part of blood) and held together by a gold pin, set with diamonds, the whole surmounted by an earl's coronet. I had taken some trouble about it, and I was grateful when Miss Dolly asked me to explain the symbolism.

"It is my heart," I observed. "The fracture is of your making: the pin—"

Here Miss Dolly interrupted; to tell the truth, I was not sorry, for I was fairly gravelled for the meaning of the pin.

"What nonsense, Mr. Carter!" said she; "but it's awfully pretty. Thanks, so very, very much. Aren't relations funny people?"

"If you wish to change the subject, pray do," said I. "I'll change anything except my affections."

CORDIAL RELATIONS

"Look here," she pursued, holding out a bundle of letters. "Here are the congratulatory epistles from relations. Shall I read you a few?"

"It will be a most agreeable mode of passing the time," said I.

"This is from Aunt Georgiana — she's a widow — lives at Cheltenham. 'My dearest Dorothea —'"

"Who?"

"Dorothea's my name, Mr. Carter. It means the gift of heaven, you know."

"Precisely. Pray proceed, Miss Dolly. I did not at first recognise you."

"'My dearest Dorothea, I have heard the news of your engagement to Lord Mickleham with deep thankfulness. To obtain the love of an honest man is a great prize. I hope you will prove worthy of it. Marriage is a trial and an opportunity —'"

"Hear, hear!" said I. "A trial for the husband and —"

"Be quiet, Mr. Carter. 'A trial and an opportunity. It searches the heart and it affords a sphere of usefulness which —' So she goes on, you know. I don't see why I need be lectured just because I'm going to be married, do you, Mr. Carter?"

"Let's try another," said I. "Who's that on pink paper?"

"Oh, that's Georgy Vane. She's awful fun. 'Dear old Dolly,—So you've brought it off. Hearty congrats. I thought you were going to be silly and throw away—' There's nothing else there, Mr. Carter. Look here. Listen to this. It's from Uncle William. He's a clergyman, you know. 'My dear Niece,—I have heard with great gratification of your engagement. Your aunt and I unite in all good wishes. I recollect Lord Mickleham's father when I held a curacy near Worcester. He was a regular attendant at church and a supporter of all good works in the diocese. If only his son takes after him' (fancy Archie!) 'you have secured a prize. I hope you have a proper sense of the responsibilities you are undertaking. Marriage affords no small opportunities; it also entails certain trials—'"

"Why, you're reading Aunt Georgiana again."

"Am I? No, it's Uncle William."

"Then let's try a fresh cast—unless you'll finish Georgy Vane's."

"Well, here's Cousin Susan's. She's an old maid, you know. It's very long. Here's a bit: 'Woman has it in her power to exercise a sacred influence. I have not the pleasure of knowing Lord Mickleham, but I hope, my dear, that you

Miss Dolly Foster

CORDIAL RELATIONS

will use your power over him for good. It is useless for me to deny that when you stayed with me, I thought you were addicted to frivolity. Doubtless marriage will sober you. Try to make a good use of its lessons. I am sending you a biscuit tin' — and so on."

"A very proper letter," said I.

Miss Dolly indulged in a slight grimace, and took up another letter.

"This," she said, "is from my sister-in-law, Mrs. Algernon Foster."

"A daughter of Lord Doldrums, wasn't she?"

"Yes. 'My dear Dorothea, — I have heard your news. I do hope it will turn out happily. I believe that any woman who *conscientiously* does her duty can find happiness in married life. Her husband and children occupy all her time and all her thoughts, and if she can look for few of the *lighter* pleasures of life, she has at least the knowledge that she is of *use* in the world. Please accept the accompanying volumes' (it's *Browning*) 'as a small — ' I say, Mr. Carter, do you think it's really like that?"

"There is still time to draw back," I observed.

"Oh, don't be silly. Here, this is my brother Tom's. 'Dear Dol, — I thought Mickleham rather an ass when I met him, but I dare say you know best. What's his place like? Does he take a moor? I thought I read that he kept a yacht. Does he? Give him my love and a kiss. Good luck, old girl.— Tom. P.S.— I'm glad it's not me, you know.'"

"A disgusting letter," I observed.

"Not at all," said Miss Dolly, dimpling. "It's just like dear old Tom. Listen to grandpapa's. ' My dear Granddaughter,— The alliance' (I rather like it's being called an alliance, Mr. Carter. It sounds like the Royal Family, does n't it?) ' you are about to contract is in all respects a suitable one. I send you my blessing, and a small check to help towards your trousseau.— Yours affectionately, Jno. Wm. Foster.'"

"That," said I, "is the best up to now."

"Yes, it's 500," said she, smiling. "Here's old Lady M.'s."

"*Whose?*" I exclaimed.

"Archie's mother's, you know. ' My dear Dorothea (as I suppose I must call you now),— Archibald has informed us of his engagement, and I and the girls' (there are five girls, Mr. Carter) ' hasten to welcome his bride. I am sure Archie will make his wife very happy. He is rather particular (like his dear father), but he has a good heart, and is not fidgety about his meals. Of course we shall be *delighted* to move out of The Towers at once. I hope we shall see a great deal

CORDIAL RELATIONS

of you soon. Archie is full of your praises, and we thoroughly trust his taste. Archie—' It's all about Archie, you see."

"Naturally," said I.

"Well, I don't know. I suppose I count a little, too. Oh, look here. Here's Cousin Fred's—but he's always so silly. I shan't read you his."

"Oh, just a bit of it," I pleaded.

"Well, here's one bit. 'I suppose I can't murder him, so I must wish him joy. All I can say is, Dolly, that he's the luckiest' (something I can't read—either fellow or—devil) 'I ever heard of. I wonder if you've forgotten that evening—'"

"Well, go on." For she stopped.

"Oh, there's nothing else."

"In fact, you have forgotten the evening?"

"Entirely," said Miss Dolly, tossing her head. "But he sends me a love of a bracelet. He can't possibly pay for it, poor boy."

"Young knave!" said I, severely. (I had paid for my pearl heart.)

"Then come a lot from girls. Oh, there's one from Maud Tottenham—she's a second cousin, you know—it's rather amusing. 'I used to know your *fiancé* slightly. He seemed very nice, but it's a long while ago, and I never saw much of him. I hope he is really fond of you, and that

THE DOLLY DIALOGUES

it is not a mere *fancy*. Since you love him so much, it would be a pity if he did not care deeply for you.'"

"Interpret, Miss Dolly," said I.

"She tried to catch him herself," said Miss Dolly.

"Ah, I see. Is that all?"

"The others are n't very interesting."

"Then let 's finish Georgy Vane's."

"Really?" she asked, smiling.

"Yes. Really."

"Oh, if you don't mind, I don't," said she, laughing, and she hunted out the pink note and spread it before her. "Let me see. Where was I? Oh, here. 'I thought you were going to be silly and throw away your chances on some of the men who used to flirt with you. Archie Mickleham may not be a genius, but he 's a good fellow and a swell and rich; he 's not a pauper, like Phil Meadows, or a snob, like Charlie Dawson, or—' *shall* I go on, Mr. Carter? No, I won't. I did n't see what it was."

"Yes, you shall go on."

"Oh, no, I can't," and she folded up the letter.

"Then I will," and I 'm ashamed to say I snatched the letter. Miss Dolly jumped to her feet. I fled behind the table. She ran round. I dodged.

CORDIAL RELATIONS

"'Or—'" I began to read.

"Stop!" cried she.

"'Or a young spendthrift like that man — I forget his name — whom you used to go on with at such a pace at Monte Carlo last winter.'"

"Stop!" she cried, stamping her foot. I read on: —

"'No doubt he was charming, my dear, and no doubt anybody would have thought you meant it; but I never doubted you. Still, weren't you just a little —'"

"Stop!" she cried. "You must stop, Mr. Carter."

So then I stopped. I folded the letter and handed it back to her. Her cheeks flushed red as she took it.

"I thought you were a gentleman," said she, biting her lip.

"I was at Monte Carlo last winter myself," said I.

"Lord Mickleham," said the butler, throwing open the door.

III
RETRIBUTION

IN future I am going to be careful what I do. I am also — and this is by no means less important — going to be very careful what Miss Dolly Foster does. Everybody knows (if I may quote her particular friend Nellie Phaeton) that dear Dolly means no harm, but she is "just a little harum-scarum." I thanked Miss Phaeton for the expression.

The fact is that "old Lady M." (here I quote Miss Dolly) sent for me the other day. I have not the honour of knowing the Countess, and I went in some trepidation. When I was ushered in, Lady Mickleham put up her "starers." (You know those abominations! *Pince-nez* with long torture — I mean tortoise — shell handles.)

"Mr. — er — Carter?" said she.

I bowed. I would have denied it if I could.

"My dears!" said Lady Mickleham.

Upon this five young ladies who had been sitting in five straight-backed chairs, doing five pieces

RETRIBUTION

of embroidery, rose, bowed, and filed out of the room. I felt very nervous. A pause followed. Then the Countess observed — and it seemed at first rather irrelevant —

"I've been reading an unpleasant story."

"In these days of French influence," I began apologetically (not that I write such stories, or indeed any stories, but Lady Mickleham invites an apologetic attitude), and my eye wandered to the table. I saw nothing worse (or better) than the morning paper there.

"Contained in a friend's letter," she continued, focussing the "starers" full on my face.

I did not know what to do, so I bowed again.

"It must have been as painful for her to write as for me to read," Lady Mickleham went on. "And that is saying much. Be seated, pray."

I bowed, and sat down in one of the straight-backed chairs. I also began, in my fright, to play with one of the pieces of embroidery.

"Is Lady Jane's work in your way?" (Lady Jane is named after Jane, the famous Countess, Lady-in-Waiting to Caroline of Anspach.)

I dropped the embroidery, and put my foot on my hat.

"I believe, Mr. Carter, that you are acquainted with Miss Dorothea Foster?"

"I have that pleasure," said I.

"Who is about to be married to my son, the Earl of Mickleham?"

"That, I believe, is so," said I. I was beginning to pull myself together.

"My son, Mr. Carter, is of a simple and trusting disposition. Perhaps I had better come to the point. I am informed by this letter that, in conversation with the writer the other day, Archibald mentioned, quite incidentally, some very startling facts. Those facts concern you, Mr. Carter."

"May I ask the name of the writer?"

"I do not think that is necessary," said she. "She is a lady in whom I have the utmost confidence."

"That is, of course, enough," said I.

"It appears, Mr. Carter — and you will excuse me if I speak plainly" — (I set my teeth) "that you have, in the first place, given to my son's bride a wedding present, which I can only describe as —"

"A pearl ornament," I interposed; "with a ruby or two, and —"

"A pearl heart," she corrected; "er — fractured, and that you explained that this absurd article represented your heart."

"Mere *badinage*," said I.

"In execrably bad taste," said she.

I bowed.

"In fact, most offensive. But that is not the

RETRIBUTION

worst. From my son's further statements it appears that on one occasion, at least, he found you and Miss Foster engaged in what I can only call — "

I raised my hand in protest. The Countess took no notice.

"What I can only call *romping*."

She shot this word at me with extraordinary violence, and when it was out she shuddered.

"Romping!" I cried.

"A thing not only atrociously vulgar at all times, but under the circumstances — need I say more? Mr. Carter, you were engaged in chasing my son's future bride round a table!"

"Pardon me, Lady Mickleham. Your son's future bride was engaged in chasing me round a table."

"It is the same thing," said Lady Mickleham.

"I should have thought there was a distinction," said I.

"None at all."

I fell back on a second line of defence.

"I didn't let her catch me, Lady Mickleham," I pleaded.

Lady Mickleham grew quite red. This made me feel more at my ease.

"No, sir. If you had — "

"Goodness knows!" I murmured, shaking my head.

"As it happened, however, my son entered in the middle of this disgraceful —"

"It was at the beginning," said I, with a regretful sigh.

Upon this — and I have really never been so pleased at anything in all my life — the Countess, the violence of her emotions penetrating to her very fingers, gripped the handle of her "starers" with such force that she broke it in two! She was a woman of the world, and in a moment she looked as if nothing had happened. With me it was different; and that I am not now on Lady Mickleham's visiting-list is due to (*inter alia et enormia*) the fact that I laughed! It was out before I could help it. In a second I was as grave as a mute. The mischief was done. The Countess rose. I imitated her example.

"You are amused?" said she, and her tones banished the last of my mirth. I stumbled on my hat, and it rolled to her feet.

"It is not probable," she observed, "that after Miss Foster's marriage you will meet her often. You will move in — er — somewhat different circles."

"I may catch a glimpse of her in her carriage from the top of my 'bus," said I.

"Your *milieu* and my son's —"

"I know his valet, though," said I.

RETRIBUTION

Lady Mickleham rang the bell. I stooped for my hat. To tell the truth, I was rather afraid to expose myself in such a defenceless attitude, but the Countess preserved her self-control. The butler opened the door. I bowed, and left the Countess regarding me through the maimed "starers." Then I found the butler smiling. He probably knew the signs of the weather. I wouldn't be Lady Mickleham's butler if you made me a duke.

As I walked home through the Park I met Miss Dolly and Mickleham. They stopped. I walked on. Mickleham seized me by the coat-tails.

"Do you mean to cut us?" he cried.

"Yes," said I.

"Why, what the deuce —?" he began.

"I've seen your mother," said I. "I wish, Mickleham, that when you do happen to intrude as you did the other day, you wouldn't repeat what you see."

"Lord!" he cried. "She's not heard of that? I only told Aunt Cynthia."

I said something about Aunt Cynthia.

"Does — does she know it *all?*" asked Miss Dolly.

"More than all — much more."

"Didn't you smooth it over?" said Miss Dolly, reproachfully.

"On reflection," said I, "I don't know that I did — much." (I had n't, you know.)

Suddenly Mickleham burst out laughing.

"What a game!" he exclaimed.

"That's all very well for you," said Dolly. "But do you happen to remember that we dine there to-night?"

Archie grew grave.

"I hope you'll enjoy yourselves," said I. "I always cling to the belief that the wicked are punished." And I looked at Miss Dolly.

"Never you mind, little woman," said Archie, drawing Miss Dolly's arm through his. "I'll see you through. After all, everybody knows that old Carter's an ass."

That piece of universal knowledge may help matters, but I do not quite see how. I walked on, for Miss Dolly had quite forgotten me, and was looking up at Archie Mickleham like — well, hang it, in the way they do, you know. So I just walked on.

I believe Miss Dolly has got a husband who is (let us say) good enough for her. And, for one reason and another, I am glad of it. And I also believe that she knows it. And I am — I suppose — glad of that too. Oh, yes, of course I am. Of course.

IV

THE PERVERSENESS OF IT

"I TELL you what, Mr. Carter," said Miss Nellie Phaeton, touching up Rhino with her whip, "love in a cottage is — "

"Lord forgive us, cinders, ashes, dust," I quoted.

We were spanking round the Park behind Ready and Rhino. Miss Phaeton's horses are very large; her groom is very small, and her courage is indomitable. I am no great hand at driving myself, and I am not always quite comfortable. Moreover, the stricter part of my acquaintance consider, I believe, that Miss Phaeton's attentions to me are somewhat pronounced, and that I ought not to drive with her in the Park.

"You're right," she went on. "What a girl wants is a good house and lots of cash, and some ridin' and a little huntin' and — "

"A few 'g's'!" I cried in shuddering entreaty. "If you love me, a 'g' or two."

"Well, I suppose so," said she. "You can't go ridin' without gees, can you?"

THE DOLLY DIALOGUES

Apparently one could go driving without any, but I did not pursue the subject.

"It's only in stories that people are in love when they marry," observed Miss Phaeton, reflectively.

"Yes, and then it's generally with somebody else," said I.

"Oh, if you count *that!*" said she, hitting Ready rather viciously. We bounded forward, and I heard the little groom bumping on the back seat. I am always glad not to be a groom — it's a cup-and-ball sort of life, which must be very wearying.

"Were you ever in love?" she asked, just avoiding a brougham which contained the Duchess of Dexminster. (If, by the way, I have to run into any one, I like it to be a Duchess: you get a much handsomer paragraph.)

"Yes," said I.

"Often?"

"Oh, not too often, and I always take great care, you know."

"What of?"

"That it shall be quite out of the question, you know. It's not at all difficult. I only have to avoid persons of moderate means."

"But aren't you a person of — ?"

"Exactly. That's why. So I choose either a

"Were you ever in Love?" she asked

THE PERVERSENESS OF IT

pauper — when it's impossible — or an heiress — when it's preposterous. See?"

"But don't you ever want to get — ?" began Miss Phaeton.

"Let's talk about something else," said I.

"I believe you're humbuggin' me," said Miss Phaeton.

"I am offering a veiled apology," said I.

"Stuff!" said she. "You know you told Dolly Foster that I should make an excellent wife for a trainer."

Oh, these women! A man had better talk to a phonograph.

"Or anybody else," said I, politely.

Miss Phaeton whipped up her horses.

"Look out! There's the mounted policeman," I cried.

"No, he isn't. Are you afraid?" she retorted.

"I'm not fit to die," I pleaded.

"I don't care a pin for your opinion, you know," she continued (I had never supposed that she did); "but what did you mean by it?"

"I never said it."

"Oh!"

"All right — I never did."

"Then Dolly invented it?"

"Of course," said I, steadily.

"On your honour?"

"Oh, come, Miss Phaeton!"

"Would — would other people think so?" she asked, with a highly surprising touch of timidity.

"Nobody would," I said. "Only a snarling old wretch would say so, just because he thought it smart."

There was a long pause. Then Miss Phaeton asked me abruptly: —

"You never met him, did you?"

"No."

A pause ensued. We passed the Duchess again, and scratched the nose of her poodle, which was looking out of the carriage window. Miss Phaeton flicked Rhino, and the groom behind went plop-plop on the seat.

"He lives in town, you know," remarked Miss Phaeton.

"They mostly do — and write about the country," said I.

"Why shouldn't they?" she asked fiercely.

"My dear Miss Phaeton, by all means let them," said I.

"He's awfully clever, you know," she continued; "but he wouldn't always talk. Sometimes he just sat and said nothin', or read a book."

A sudden intuition discovered Mr. Gay's feelings to me.

THE PERVERSENESS OF IT

"You were talking about the run, or something, I suppose?"

"Yes, or the bag, you know."

As she spoke, she pulled up Ready and Rhino. The little groom jumped down and stood under (not at) their heads. I leant back and surveyed the crowd sitting and walking. Miss Phaeton flicked a fly off Rhino's ear, put her whip in the socket, and leant back also.

"Then I suppose you did n't care much about him?" I asked.

"Oh, I liked him pretty well," she answered very carelessly.

At this moment, looking along the walk, I saw a man coming towards us. He was a handsome fellow, with just a touch of " softness " in his face. He was dressed in correct fashion, save that his hair was a trifle longer, his coat a trifle fuller, his hat a trifle larger, his tie a trifle looser than they were worn by most. He caught my attention, and I went on looking at him for a little while, till a slight movement of my companion's made me turn my head.

Miss Phaeton was sitting bolt upright: she fidgeted with the reins; she took her whip out of the socket and put it back again; and, to my amazement, her cheeks were very red.

Presently the man came opposite the carriage. Miss Phaeton bowed. He lifted his hat, smiled, and made as if to pass on. Miss Phaeton held out her hand. I could see a momentary gleam of surprise in his eye, as though he thought her cordiality more than he might have looked for — possibly even more than he cared about. But he stopped and shook hands.

"How are you, Mr. Gay?" she said, not introducing me.

"Still with your inseparables!" he said gaily, with a wave of his hand towards the horses. "I hope, Miss Phaeton, that in the next world your faithful steeds will be allowed to bear you company, or what will you do?"

"Oh, you think I care for nothin' but horses?" said she, petulantly, but she leant towards him, and gave me her shoulder.

"Oh, no," he laughed. "Dogs also, and I'm afraid one day it was ferrets, was n't it?"

"Have — have you written any poetry lately?" she asked.

"How conscientious of you to inquire!" he exclaimed, his eyes twinkling. "Oh, yes, half a hundred things. Have you — killed — anything lately?"

I could swear she flushed again. Her voice trembled as she answered, —

"No, not lately."

I caught sight of his face behind her back, and I

THE PERVERSENESS OF IT

thought I saw a trace of puzzle — nothing more. He held out his hand.

"Well, so glad to have seen you, Miss Phaeton," said he, "but I must run on. Good-by."

"Good-by, Mr. Gay," said she.

And, lifting his hat again, smiling again gaily, he was gone. For a moment or two I said nothing. Then I remarked, —

"So that's your friend Gay, is it? He's not a bad-looking fellow."

"Yes, that's him," said she, and, as she spoke, she sank back in her seat for a moment. I did not look at her face. Then she sat up straight again and took the whip.

"Want to stay any longer?" she asked.

"No," said I.

The little groom sprang away, Rhino and Ready dashed ahead.

"Shall I drop you at the club?" she asked. "I'm goin' home."

"I'll get out here," said I.

We came to a stand again, and I got down.

"Good-by," I said.

She nodded at me, but said nothing. A second later the carriage was tearing down the road, and the little groom hanging on for dear life.

Of course it's all nonsense. She's not the least suited to him; she'd make him miserable, and then be miserable herself. But it seems a little perverse, does n't it? In fact, twice at least between the courses at dinner I caught myself being sorry for her. It is, when you think of it, so remarkably perverse.

V

A MATTER OF DUTY

LADY MICKLEHAM is back from her honeymoon. I mean young Lady Mickleham— Dolly Foster (well, of course I do. Fancy the Dowager on a honeymoon!). She signified the fact to me by ordering me to call on her at tea-time; she had, she said, something which she wished to consult me about *confidentially*. I went.

"I did n't know you were back," I observed.

"Oh, we 've been back a fortnight, but we went down to The Towers. They were all there, Mr. Carter."

"All who?"

"All Archie's people. The Dowager said we must get really to know one another as soon as possible. I 'm not sure I like really knowing people. It means that they say whatever they like to you, and don't get up out of your favourite chair when you come in."

"I agree," said I, "that a *soupçon* of unfamiliarity is not amiss."

"Of course it's nice to be one of the family," she continued.

"The cat is that," said I. "I would not give a fig for it."

"And the Dowager taught me the ways of the house."

"Ah, she taught me the way out of it."

"And showed me how to be most disagreeable to the servants."

"It is the first lesson of a housekeeper."

"And told me what Archie particularly liked, and how bad it was for him, poor boy."

"What should we do without our mothers? I do not, however, see how I can help in all this, Lady Mickleham."

"How funny that sounds!"

"Aren't you accustomed to your dignity yet?"

"I meant from *you*, Mr. Carter."

I smiled. That is Dolly's way. As Miss Phaeton says, she means no harm, and it is admirably conducive to the pleasure of a *tête-à-tête*.

"It wasn't that I wanted to ask you about," she continued, after she had indulged in a pensive sigh (with a dutifully bright smile and a glance at Archie's photograph to follow. Her behaviour always reminds me of a varied and well-assorted *menu*). "It was about something much more difficult. You won't tell Archie, will you?"

"Are n't you accustomed to your dignity yet?"

A MATTER OF DUTY

"This becomes interesting," I remarked, putting my hat down.

"You know, Mr. Carter, that before I was married — oh, how long ago it seems!"

"Not at all."

"Don't interrupt. That before I was married I had several — that is to say, several — well, several —"

"Start quite afresh," I suggested encouragingly.

"Well, then, several men were silly enough to think themselves — you know."

"No one better," I assented cheerfully.

"Oh, if you won't be sensible! — Well, you see, many of them are Archie's friends as well as mine; and, of course, they've been to call."

"It is but good manners," said I.

"One of them waited to be sent for, though."

"Leave that fellow out," said I.

"What I want to ask you is this — and I believe you're not silly, really, you know, except when you choose to be."

"Walk in the Row any afternoon," said I, "and you won't find ten wiser men."

"It's this. Ought I to tell Archie?"

"Good gracious! Here's a problem!"

"Of course," pursued Lady Mickleham, opening her fan, "it's in some ways more comfortable that he shouldn't know."

"For him?"

"Yes — and for me. But then it does n't seem quite fair."

"To him?"

"Yes — and to me. Because if he came to know from anybody else, he might exaggerate the things, you know."

"Impossible!"

"Mr. Carter!"

"I — er — mean he knows you too well to do such a thing."

"Oh, I see. Thank you. Yes. What do you think?"

"What does the Dowager say?"

"I have n't mentioned it to the Dowager."

"But surely, on such a point, her experience —"

"She can't have any," said Lady Mickleham, decisively. "I believe in her husband, because I must. But nobody else! You 're not giving me your opinion."

I reflected for a moment.

"Have n't we left out one point of view?" I ventured to suggest.

"I 've thought it all over very carefully," said she; "both as it would affect me and as it would affect Archie."

"Quite so. Now suppose you think how it would affect them!"

A MATTER OF DUTY

"Who?"

"Why, the men."

Lady Mickleham put down her cup of tea.

"What a very curious idea!" she exclaimed.

"Give it time to sink in," said I, helping myself to another piece of toast.

She sat silent for a few moments — presumably to allow of the permeation I suggested. I finished my tea and leant back comfortably. Then I said, —

"Let me take my own case. Shouldn't I feel rather awkward — ?"

"Oh, it's no good taking your case," she interrupted.

"Why not mine as well as another?"

"Because I told him about you long ago."

I was not surprised. But I could not permit Lady Mickleham to laugh at me in the unconscionable manner in which she proceeded to laugh. I spread out my hands and observed blandly, —

"Why not be guided — as to the others, I mean — by your husband's example?"

"Archie's example? What's that?"

"I don't know; but you do, I suppose."

"What do you mean, Mr. Carter?" she asked, sitting upright.

"Well, has he ever told you about Maggie Adeane?"

"I never heard of her."
"Or Lilly Courtenay?"
"*That* girl!"
"Or Alice Layton?"
"The red-haired Layton?"
"Or Florence Cunliffe?"
"Who was she?"
"Or Millie Trehearne?"
"She squints, Mr. Carter."
"Or—"

"Stop, stop! What do you mean? What should he tell me?"

"Oh, I see he has n't. Nor, I suppose, about Sylvia Fenton, or that little Delancy girl, or handsome Miss — what was her name?"

"Hold your tongue — and tell me what you mean."

"Lady Mickleham," said I, gravely, "if your husband has not thought fit to mention these ladies — and others whom I could name — to you, how could I presume—?"

"Do you mean to tell me that Archie—?"

"He'd only known you three years, you see."

"Then it was before—?"

"Some of them were before," said I.

Lady Mickleham drew a long breath.

"Archie will be in soon," said she.

I took my hat.

A MATTER OF DUTY

"It seems to me," I observed, "that what is sauce — that, I should say, husband and wife ought to stand on an equal footing in these matters. Since he has — no doubt for good reasons — not mentioned to you —"

"Alice Layton was a positive fright."

"She came last," said I. "Just before you, you know. However, as I was saying —"

"And that horrible Sylvia Fenton —"

"Oh, he could n't have known you long then. As I was saying, I should, if I were you, treat him as he has treated you. In my case it seems to be too late."

"I 'm sorry I told him that."

"Oh, pray don't mind, it's of no consequence. As to the others —"

"I should never have thought it of Archie!"

"One never knows," said I, with an apologetic smile. "I don't suppose he thinks it of you."

"I won't tell him a single word. He may find out if he likes. Who was the last girl you mentioned?"

"Is it any use trying to remember all their names?" I asked in a soothing tone. "No doubt he's forgotten them by now — just as you 've forgotten the others."

"And the Dowager told me that he had never had an attachment before."

"Oh, if the Dowager said that! Of course, the Dowager would know!"

"Don't be so silly, for goodness' sake! Are you going?"

"Certainly I am. It might annoy Archie to find me here when he wants to talk to you."

"Well, I want to talk to him."

"Of course you won't repeat what I've —"

"I shall find out for myself," she said.

"Good-by. I hope I've removed all your troubles?"

"Oh, yes, thank you. I know what to do now, Mr. Carter."

"Always send for me if you're in any trouble. I have some exp —"

"Good-by, Mr. Carter."

"Good-by, Lady Mickleham. And remember that Archie, like you —"

"Yes, yes; I know. Must you go?"

"I'm afraid I must. I've enjoyed our talk so —"

"There's Archie's step."

I left the room. On the stairs I met Archie. I shook hands sympathetically. I was sorry for Archie. But in great causes the individual cannot be considered. I had done my duty to my sex.

VI

MY LAST CHANCE

"NOW mind," said Mrs. Hilary Musgrave, impressively, "this is the last time I shall take any trouble about you. She's a very nice girl, quite pretty, and she'll have a lot of money. You can be very pleasant when you like —"

"This unsolicited testimonial —"

"Which isn't often — and if you don't do it this time I wash my hands of you. Why, how old are you?"

"Hush, Mrs. Hilary."

"You must be nearly —"

"It's false — false — false!"

"Come along," said Mrs. Hilary, and she added, over her shoulder, "she has a slight north-country accent."

"It might have been Scotch," said I.

"She plays the piano a good deal."

"It might have been the fiddle," said I.

"She's very fond of Browning."

"It might have been Ibsen," said I.

THE DOLLY DIALOGUES

Mrs. Hilary, seeing that I was determined to look on the bright side, smiled graciously on me and introduced me to the young lady. She was decidedly good-looking, fresh and sincere of aspect, with large inquiring eyes — eyes which I felt would demand a little too much of me at breakfast — but then a large tea-urn puts that all right.

"Miss Sophia Milton — Mr. Carter," said Mrs. Hilary, and left us.

Well, we tried the theatres first; but as she had only been to the Lyceum and I had only been to the Gaiety, we soon got to the end of that. Then we tried Art: she asked me what I thought of Degas: I evaded the question by criticising a drawing of a horse in last week's "Punch" — which she had n't seen. Upon this she started literature. She said "Some Qualms and a Shiver" was the book of the season. I put my money on "The Queen of the Quorn." Dead stop again! And I saw Mrs. Hilary's eye upon me: there was wrath in her face. Something must be done.

A brilliant idea seized me. I had read that four-fifths of the culture of England were Conservative. I also was a Conservative. It was four to one on! I started politics. I could have whooped for joy when I elicited something particularly incisive about the ignorance of the masses.

MY LAST CHANCE

"I do hope you agree with me," said Miss Milton. "The more one reads and thinks, the more one sees how fatally false a theory it is that the ignorant masses — people such as I have described — can ever rule a great Empire."

"The Empire wants gentlemen; that's what it wants," said I, nodding my head, and glancing triumphantly at Mrs. Hilary.

"Men and women," said she, "who are acquainted with the best that has been said and thought on all important subjects."

At the time I believed this observation to be original, but I have since been told that it was borrowed. I was delighted with it.

"Yes," said I, "and have got a stake in the country, you know, and know how to behave 'emselves in the House, don't you know?"

"What we have to do," pursued Miss Milton, "is to guide the voters. These poor rustics need to be informed —"

"Just so," I broke in. "They have to be told —"

"Of the real nature of the questions —"

"And which candidate to support."

"Or they must infallibly —" she exclaimed.

"Get their marching orders," I cried, in rapture. It was exactly what I always did on my small property.

"Oh, I did n't quite mean that," she said reproachfully.

"Oh, well, neither did I — quite," I responded adroitly. What was wrong with the girl now?

"But with the help of the League —" she went on.

"Do you belong?" I cried, more delighted than ever.

"Oh, yes!" said she. "I think it's a duty. I worked very hard at the last election. I spent days distributing packages of —"

Then I made, I'm sorry to say, a false step. I observed, interrupting, —

"But it's ticklish work now, eh? Six months' 'hard' would n't be pleasant, would it?"

"What do you mean, Mr. — er — Carter?" she asked.

I was still blind. I believe I winked, and I'm sure I whispered, "*Tea*."

Miss Milton drew herself up very straight.

"I do not *bribe*," she said. "What I distribute is pamphlets."

Now, I suppose that "pamphlets" and "blankets" don't really sound much alike, but I was agitated.

"Quite right," said I. "Poor old things! They can't afford proper fuel."

She rose to her feet.

MY LAST CHANCE

"I should think not, Miss Milton," said I, admiringly.

"Oh, I should like to meet that man, and tell him what I think of him!" said she. "Such men as he is do more harm than a dozen agitators. So contemptible, too!"

"It's revolting to think of," said I.

"I'm *so* glad you —" began Miss Milton quite confidentially; I pulled my chair a trifle closer, and cast an apparently careless glance towards Mrs. Hilary. Suddenly I heard a voice behind me.

"Eh, what? Upon my honour it is! Why, Carter, my boy, how are you? Eh, what? Miss Milton, too, I declare!' Well, now, what a pity Annie did n't come!"

I disagreed. I hate Annie. But I was very glad to see my friend and neighbour, Robert Dinnerly. He's a sensible man — his wife's a little prig.

"Oh, Mr. Dinnerly," cried Miss Milton, "how funny that you should come just now! I was just trying to remember the name of a man Mrs. Dinnerly told me about. I was telling Mr. Carter about him. You know him."

"Well, Miss Milton, perhaps I do. Describe him."

"I don't believe Annie ever told me his name, but she was talking about him at our house yesterday."

"But I wasn't there, Miss Milton."

"No," said Miss Milton, "but he's got the next place to yours in the country."

I positively leapt from my seat.

"Why, good gracious, Carter himself, you mean!" cried Dinnerly, laughing. "Well, that is a good 'un — ha-ha-ha!"

She turned a stony glare on me.

"Do you live next to Mr. Dinnerly in the country?" she asked.

I would have denied it if Dinnerly had not been there. As it was I blew my nose.

"I wonder," said Miss Milton, "what has become of Aunt Emily."

"Miss Milton," said I, "by a happy chance you have enjoyed a luxury. You have told the man what you think of him."

"Yes," said she; "and I have only to add that he is also a hypocrite."

Pleasant, wasn't it? Yet Mrs. Hilary says it was my fault! That's a woman all over!

VII

THE LITTLE WRETCH!

SEEING that little Johnny Tompkins was safely out of the country, under injunctions to make a new man of himself, and to keep that new man, when made, at the Antipodes, I could not see anything indiscreet in touching on the matter in the course of conversation with Mrs. Hilary Musgrave. In point of fact, I was curious to find out what she knew, and, supposing she knew, what she thought. So I mentioned little Johnny Tompkins.

"Oh, the little wretch!" cried Mrs. Hilary. "You know he came here two or three times? Anybody can impose on Hilary."

"Happy woman! I — I mean unhappy man, Mrs. Hilary."

"And how much was it he stole?"

"Hard on a thousand," said I. "For a time, you know, he was quite a man of fashion."

"Oh, I know. He came here in his own hansom, perfectly dressed, and —"

"Behaved all right, did n't he?"

"Yes. Of course there was a something."

"Or you would n't have been deceived!" said I, with a smile.

"I was n't deceived," said Mrs. Hilary, an admirable flush appearing on her cheeks.

"That is to say, Hilary would n't."

"Oh, Hilary! Why did n't his employers prosecute him, Mr. Carter?"

"In the first place, he had that inestimable advantage in a career of dishonesty, — respectable relations."

"Well, but still —"

"His widowed mother was a trump, you know."

"Do you mean a good woman?"

"Doubtless she was; but I meant a good card. However, there was another reason."

"I can't see any," declared Mrs. Hilary.

"I'm going to surprise you," said I. "Hilary interceded for him."

"Hilary?"

"You did n't know it? I thought not. Well, he did."

"Why, he always pretended to want him to be convicted."

"Cunning Hilary!" said I.

"He used to speak most strongly against him."

"That was his guile," said I.

THE LITTLE WRETCH!

"Oh, but why in the world—?" she began; then she paused, and went on again: "It was nothing to do with Hilary."

"Hilary went with me to see him, you know, while they had him under lock and key at the firm's offices."

"Did he? I never heard that."

"And he was much impressed with his bearing."

"Well, I suppose, Mr. Carter, that if he was really penitent—"

"Never saw a man less penitent," I interrupted. "He gloried in his crime; if I remember his exact expression, it was that the jam was jolly well worth the powder, and if they liked to send him to chokee, they could and be—and suffer accordingly, you know."

"And after that, Hilary—!"

"Oh, anybody can impose on Hilary, you know. Hilary only asked what 'the jam' was."

"It's a horrid expression, but I suppose it meant acting the part of a gentleman, did n't it?"

"Not entirely. According to what he told Hilary, Johnny was in love."

"Oh, and he stole for some wretched—?"

"Now, do be careful. What do you know about the lady?"

"The *lady!* I can imagine Johnny Tompkins' ideal!"

"So can I, if you come to that."

"And she must have known his money was n't his own."

"Why must she?" I asked. "According to what he told Hilary, she did n't."

"I don't believe it," said Mrs. Hilary, with decision.

"Hilary believed it!"

"Oh, Hilary!"

"But then, Hilary knew the girl."

"Hilary knew—! You mean to say Hilary knew—?"

"No one better," said I, composedly.

Mrs. Hilary rose to her feet.

"Who was the creature?" she asked sharply.

"Come," I expostulated, "how would you like it, if your young man had taken to theft, and—"

"Oh, nonsense. Tell me her name, please, Mr. Carter."

"Johnny told Hilary that just to see her and talk to her and sit by her was 'worth all the money'—but, then, to be sure, it was somebody else's money—and that he'd do it again to get what he had got over again. Then, I'm sorry to say, he swore."

"And Hilary believed that stuff?"

"Hilary agreed with him," said I. "Hilary, you see, knows the lady."

THE LITTLE WRETCH!

"What's her name, Mr. Carter?"

"Did n't you notice his attentions to any one?"

"I notice! You don't mean that I 've seen her?"

"Certainly you have."

"Was she ever here?"

"Yes, Mrs. Hilary. Hilary takes care of that."

"I shall be angry in a minute, Mr. Carter. Oh, I 'll have this out of Hilary!"

"I should."

"Who was she?"

"According to what he told Hilary, she was the most fascinating woman in the world. Hilary thought so, too."

Mrs. Hilary began to walk up and down.

"Oh, so Hilary helped to let him go, because they both — ?"

"Precisely," said I.

"And you dare to come and tell me?"

"Well, I thought you ought to know," said I. "Hilary's just as mad about her as Johnny — in fact, he said he 'd be hanged if he would n't have done the same himself."

I have once seen Madame Ristori play Lady Macbeth. Her performance was recalled to me by the tones in which Mrs. Hilary asked:

"Who is this woman, if you please, Mr. Carter?"

"So Hilary got him off — gave him fifty pounds too."

"Glad to get him away, perhaps," she burst out, in angry scorn.

"Who knows?" said I. "Perhaps."

"Her name?" demanded Lady Macbeth — I mean Mrs. Hilary — again.

"I shan't tell you, unless you promise to say nothing to Hilary."

"To say nothing! Well, really — "

"Oh, all right!" and I took up my hat.

"But I can watch them, can't I?"

"As much as you like."

"Won't you tell me?"

"If you promise."

"Well, then, I promise."

"Look in the glass."

"What for?"

"To see your face, to be sure."

She started, blushed red, and moved a step towards me.

"You don't mean — ?" she cried.

"Thou art the woman," said I.

"Oh, but he never said a word — "

"Johnny had his code," said I. "And in some ways it was better than some people's, — in some, alas! worse."

"And Hilary?"

"Really you know better than I do whether I've told the truth about Hilary."

THE LITTLE WRETCH!

A pause ensued. Then Mrs. Hilary made three short remarks, which I give in their order:—

(1) "The little wretch!"
(2) "Dear old Hilary!"
(3) "Poor little man!"

I took my hat. I knew that Hilary was due from the City in a few minutes. Mrs. Hilary sat down by the fire.

"How dare you torment me so?" she asked, but not in the least like Lady Macbeth.

"I must have my little amusements," said I.

"What an audacious little creature!" said Mrs. Hilary. "Fancy his daring!—Are n't you astounded?"

"Oh, yes, I am. But Hilary, you see—"

"It's nearly his time," said Mrs. Hilary.

I buttoned my left glove and held out my right hand.

"I've a good mind not to shake hands with you," said she. "Was n't it absurd of Hilary?"

"Horribly."

"He ought to have been all the more angry."

"Of course he ought."

"The presumption of it!" And Mrs. Hilary smiled. I also smiled.

"That poor old mother of his," reflected Mrs. Hilary. "Where did you say she lived?"

"Hilary knows the address," said I.

THE DOLLY DIALOGUES

"Silly little wretch!" mused Mrs. Hilary, still smiling.

"Good-by," said I.

"Good-by," said Mrs. Hilary.

I turned towards the door and had laid my hand on the knob, when Mrs. Hilary called softly, —

"Mr. Carter."

"Yes," said I, turning.

"Do you know where the little wretch has gone?"

"Oh, yes," said I.

"I — I suppose you don't ever write to him?"

"Dear me, no," said I.

"But you — could?" suggested Mrs. Hilary.

"Of course," said I.

She jumped up and ran towards me. Her purse was in one hand, and a bit of paper fluttered in the other.

"Send him that — don't tell him," she whispered, and her voice had a little catch in it. "Poor little wretch!" said she.

As for me, I smiled cynically — quite cynically, you know: for it was very absurd.

"Please go," said Mrs. Hilary.

And I went.

Supposing it had been another woman! Well, I wonder!

VIII

AN EXPENSIVE PRIVILEGE

A RATHER uncomfortable thing happened the other day which threatened a schism in my acquaintance and put me in a decidedly awkward position. It was no other than this: Mrs. Hilary Musgrave had definitely informed me that she did not approve of Lady Mickleham. The attitude is, no doubt, a conceivable one, but I was surprised that a woman of Mrs. Hilary's large sympathies should adopt it. Besides, Mrs. Hilary is quite good-looking herself.

The history of the affair is much as follows: I called on Mrs. Hilary to see whether I could do anything, and she told me all about it. It appears that Mrs. Hilary had a bad cold and a cousin up from the country about the same time (she was justly aggrieved at the double event), and, being unable to go to the Duchess of Dexminster's "squash," she asked Dolly Mickleham to chaperon little Miss Phyllis. Little Miss Phyllis, of course, knew no one there, — the Duchess least of all (but then very few of us — yes, I was there — knew the Duchess, and the Duchess did n't know any of us; I saw her shake hands with a waiter myself, just to be on the safe side), — and an hour after the party began, she was discovered wandering about in a most desolate condition. Dolly had told her that she would be in a certain place; and when Miss Phyllis came Dolly was not there. The poor little lady wandered about for another hour, looking so lost that one was inclined to send for a policeman; and then she sat down on a seat by the wall, and in desperation asked her next-door neighbour if he knew Lady Mickleham by sight, and had he seen her lately. The next-door neighbour, by way of reply, called out to a quiet elderly gentleman who was sidling unobtrusively about, "Duke, are there any particularly snug corners in your house?" The Duke stopped, searched his memory, and said that at the end of the Red Corridor there was a passage; and that a few yards down the passage, if you turned very suddenly to the right, you would come on a little nook under the stairs. The little nook just held a settee, and the settee (the Duke thought) might just hold two people. The next-door neighbour thanked the Duke, and observed to Miss Phyllis, —

AN EXPENSIVE PRIVILEGE

"It will give me great pleasure to take you to Lady Mickleham." So they went, it being then, according to Miss Phyllis's sworn statement, precisely two hours and five minutes since Dolly had disappeared; and, pursuing the route indicated by the Duke, they found Lady Mickleham. And Lady Mickleham exclaimed, "Good gracious, my dear, I'd quite forgotten you! Have you had an ice? Do take her to have an ice, Sir John." (Sir John Berry was the next-door neighbour.) And with that Lady Mickleham is said to have resumed her conversation.

"Did you ever hear anything more atrocious?" concluded Mrs. Hilary. "I really cannot think what Lord Mickleham is doing."

"You surely mean, what Lady Mickleham —?"

"No, I don't," said Mrs. Hilary, with extraordinary decision. "Anything might have happened to that poor child."

"Oh, there were not many of the aristocracy present," said I, soothingly.

"But it's not that so much, as the thing itself. She's the most disgraceful flirt in London."

"How do you know she was flirting?" I inquired with a smile.

"How do I know?" echoed Mrs. Hilary.

"It is a very hasty conclusion," I persisted. "Sometimes I stay talking with you for an hour or more. Are you, therefore, flirting with me?"

"With *you!*" exclaimed Mrs. Hilary, with a little laugh.

"Absurd as the supposition is," I remarked, "it yet serves to point the argument. Lady Mickleham might have been talking with a friend just in the quiet, rational way in which we are talking now."

"I don't think that's likely," said Mrs. Hilary; and — well, I do not like to say that she sniffed — it would convey too strong an idea, but she did make an odd little sound something like a much etherealised sniff.

I smiled again, and more broadly. I was enjoying beforehand the little victory which I was to enjoy over Mrs. Hilary.

"Yet it happens to be true," said I.

Mrs. Hilary was magnificently contemptuous.

"Lord Mickleham told you so, I suppose?" she asked. "And I suppose Lady Mickleham told him — poor man!"

"Why do you call him 'poor man'?"

"Oh, never mind. Did he tell you?"

"Certainly not. The fact is, Mrs. Hilary — and really, you must excuse me for having kept you in the dark a little — it amused me so much to hear your suspicions."

"*Why, I was the man with Lady Mickleham*"

AN EXPENSIVE PRIVILEGE

Mrs. Hilary rose to her feet.

"Well, what are you going to say?" she asked.

I laughed, as I answered, —

"Why, I was the man with Lady Mickleham when your friend and Berry inter — when they arrived, you know."

Well, I should have thought — I should still think — that she would have been pleased — relieved, you know — to find her uncharitable opinion erroneous, and pleased to have it altered on the best authority. I'm sure that is how I should have felt. It was not, however, how Mrs. Hilary felt.

"I am deeply pained," she observed after a long pause; and then she held out her hand.

"I was sure you'd forgive my little deception," said I, grasping it. I thought still that she meant to bury all unkindness.

"I should never have thought it of you," she went on.

"I didn't know your friend was there at all," I pleaded; for by now I was alarmed.

"Oh, please don't shuffle like that," said Mrs. Hilary.

She continued to stand, and I rose to my feet. Mrs. Hilary held out her hand again.

"Do you mean that I'm to go?" said I.

"I hope we shall see you again some day," said

THE DOLLY DIALOGUES

Mrs. Hilary; the tone suggested that she was looking forward to some future existence, when my earthly sins should have been sufficiently purged. It reminded me for the moment of King Arthur and Queen Guinevère.

"But I protest," I began, "that my only object in telling you was to show you how absurd —"

"Is it any good talking about it now?" asked Mrs. Hilary. A discussion might possibly be fruitful in the dim futurity before mentioned — but not now — that was what she seemed to say.

"Lady Mickleham and I, on the occasion in question —" I began, with dignity.

"Pray spare me," quoth Mrs. Hilary, with much greater dignity.

I took my hat.

"Shall you be at home as usual on Thursday?" I asked.

"I have a great many people coming already," she remarked.

"I can take a hint," said I.

"I wish you'd take warning," said Mrs. Hilary.

"I will take my leave," said I; and I did, leaving Mrs. Hilary in a tragic attitude in the middle of the room. Never again shall I go out of my way to lull Mrs. Hilary's suspicions.

A day or two after this very trying interview, Lady Mickleham's victoria happened to stop

AN EXPENSIVE PRIVILEGE

opposite where I was seated in the park. I went to pay my respects.

"Do you mean to leave me nothing in the world," I asked, just by way of introducing the subject of Mrs. Hilary. "One of my best friends has turned me out of her house on your account."

"Oh, do tell me," said Dolly, dimpling all over her face.

So I told her; I made the story as long as I could for reasons connected with the dimples.

"What fun!" exclaimed Dolly. "I told you at the time that a young unmarried person like you ought to be more careful."

"I am just debating," I observed, "whether to sacrifice you."

"To sacrifice me, Mr. Carter?"

"Of course," I explained; "if I dropped you, Mrs. Hilary would let me come again."

"How charming that would be!" cried Dolly. "You would enjoy her nice serious conversation—all about Hilary!"

"She is apt," I conceded, "to touch on Hilary. But she is very picturesque."

"Oh, yes, she's handsome," said Dolly.

There was a pause. Then Dolly said, "Well?"

"Well?" said I in return.

"Is it good-by?" asked Dolly, drawing down the corners of her mouth.

"It comes to this," I remarked. "Supposing I forgive you—"

"As if it was my fault!"

"And risk Mrs. Hilary's wrath—did you speak?"

"No; I laughed, Mr. Carter."

"What shall I get out of it?"

The sun was shining brightly: it shone on Dolly; she had raised her parasol, but she blinked a little beneath it. She was smiling slightly still, and one dimple stuck to its post—like a sentinel, ready to rouse the rest from their brief repose. Dolly lay back in the victoria, nestling luxuriously against the soft cushions. She turned her eyes for a moment on me.

"Why are you looking at me?" she asked.

"Because," said I, "there is nothing better to look at."

"Do you like doing it?" asked Dolly.

"It is a privilege," said I, politely.

"Well, then!" said Dolly.

"But," I ventured to observe, "it's rather an expensive one."

"Then you mustn't have it very often."

"And it is shared by so many people."

"Then," said Dolly, smiling indulgently, "you must have it—a little oftener. Home, Roberts, please."

I am not yet allowed at Mrs. Hilary Musgrave's.

IX

A VERY DULL AFFAIR

"TO hear you talk," remarked Mrs. Hilary Musgrave — and, if any one is surprised to find me at her house, I can only say that Hilary, when he asked me to take pot-luck, was quite ignorant of any ground of difference between his wife and myself, and that Mrs. Hilary could not very well eject me on my arrival in evening dress at ten minutes to eight — "to hear you talk one would think that there was no such thing as real love."

She paused. I smiled.

"Now," she continued, turning a fine, but scornful eye upon me, "I have never cared for any man in the world except my husband."

I smiled again. Poor Hilary looked very uncomfortable. With an apologetic air he began to stammer something about Parish Councils. I was not to be diverted by any such manœuvre. It was impossible that he could really wish to talk on that subject.

"Would a person who had never eaten anything but beef make a boast of it?" I asked.

Hilary grinned covertly. Mrs. Hilary pulled the lamp nearer, and took up her embroidery.

"Do you always work the same pattern?" said I.

Hilary kicked me gently. Mrs. Hilary made no direct reply, but presently she began to talk.

"I was just about Phyllis's age"—(by the way, little Miss Phyllis was there)—"when I first saw Hilary. You remember, Hilary? At Bournemouth?"

"Oh—er—was it Bournemouth?" said Hilary, with much carelessness.

"I was on the pier," pursued Mrs. Hilary. "I had a red frock on, I remember, and one of those big hats they wore that year. Hilary wore—"

"Blue serge," I interpolated, encouragingly.

"Yes, blue serge," said she, fondly. "He had been yachting, and he was beautifully burnt. I was horribly burnt—was n't I, Hilary?"

Hilary began to pat the dog.

"Then we got to know one another."

"Stop a minute," said I. "How did that happen?"

Mrs. Hilary blushed.

"Well, we were both always on the pier," she explained. "And—and somehow Hilary got to

A VERY DULL AFFAIR

know father, and — and father introduced him to me."

"I'm glad it was no worse," said I. I was considering Miss Phyllis, who sat listening, open-eyed.

"And then, you know, father wasn't always there; and once or twice we met on the cliff. Do you remember that morning, Hilary?"

"What morning?" asked Hilary, patting the dog with immense assiduity.

"Why, the morning I had my white serge on. I'd been bathing, and my hair was down to dry, and you said I looked like a mermaid."

"Do mermaids wear white serge?" I asked; but nobody took the least notice of me — quite properly.

"And you told me such a lot about yourself; and then we found we were late for lunch."

"Yes," said Hilary, suddenly forgetting the dog, "and your mother gave me an awful glance."

"Yes, and then you told me that you were very poor, but that you couldn't help it; and you said you supposed I couldn't possibly —"

"Well, I didn't think — !"

"And I said you were a silly old thing; and then —" Mrs. Hilary stopped abruptly.

"How lovely!" remarked little Miss Phyllis, in a wistful voice.

"And do you remember," pursued Mrs. Hilary, laying down her embroidery and clasping her hands on her knees, "the morning you went to see father?"

"What a row there was!" said Hilary.

"And what an awful week it was after that! I was never so miserable in all my life. I cried till my eyes were quite red, and then I bathed them for an hour, and then I went to the pier, and you were there — and I might n't speak to you!"

"I remember," said Hilary, nodding gently.

"And then, Hilary, father sent for me and told me it was no use; and I said I 'd never marry any one else. And father said, 'There, there, don't cry. We 'll see what mother says.'"

"Your mother was a brick," said Hilary, poking the fire.

"And that night — they never told me anything about it, and I did n't even change my frock, but came down, looking horrible, just as I was, in an old black rag — Now, Hilary, don't say it was pretty!"

Hilary, unconvinced, shook his head.

"And when I walked into the drawing-room there was nobody there but just you; and we neither of us said anything for ever so long. And then father and mother came in and — do you remember after dinner, Hilary?"

A VERY DULL AFFAIR

"I remember," said Hilary.

There was a long pause. Mrs. Hilary was looking into the fire; little Miss Phyllis's eyes were fixed, in rapt gaze, on the ceiling; Hilary was looking at his wife; I, thinking it safest, was regarding my own boots.

At last Miss Phyllis broke the silence.

"How perfectly lovely!" she said.

"Yes," said Mrs. Hilary. "And we were married three months afterwards."

"Tenth of June," said Hilary, reflectively.

"And we had the most charming little rooms in the world! Do you remember those first rooms, dear? So tiny!"

"Not bad little rooms," said Hilary.

"How awfully lovely!" cried little Miss Phyllis.

I felt that it was time to interfere.

"And is that all?" I asked.

"All? How do you mean?" said Mrs. Hilary, with a slight start.

"Well, I mean, did nothing else happen? Were n't there any complications? Were n't there any more troubles, or any more opposition, or any misunderstandings, or anything?"

"No," said Mrs. Hilary.

"You never quarrelled, or broke it off?"

"No."

"Nobody came between you?"

"No. It all went just perfectly. Why, of course it did."

"Hilary's people made themselves nasty, perhaps?" I suggested, with a ray of hope.

"They fell in love with her on the spot," said Hilary.

Then I rose and stood with my back to the fire.

"I do not know," I observed, "what Miss Phyllis thinks about it—"

"I think it was just perfect, Mr. Carter."

"But for my part, I can only say that I never heard of such a dull affair in all my life."

"*Dull!*" gasped Miss Phyllis.

"*Dull!*" murmured Mrs. Hilary.

"*Dull!*" chuckled Hilary.

"It was," said I, severely, "without a spark of interest from beginning to end. Such things happen by thousands. It's commonplaceness itself. I had some hopes when your father assumed a firm attitude, but—"

"Mother was such a dear," interrupted Mrs. Hilary.

"Just so. She gave away the whole situation. Then I did trust that Hilary would lose his place, or develop an old flame, or do something just a little interesting."

"It was a perfect time," said Mrs. Hilary.

"I wonder why in the world you told me about it," I pursued.

A VERY DULL AFFAIR

"I don't know why I did," said Mrs. Hilary, dreamily.

"The only possible excuse for an engagement like that," I observed, "is to be found in intense post-nuptial unhappiness."

Hilary rose, and advanced towards his wife.

"Your embroidery's falling on the floor," said he.

"Not a bit of it," said I.

"Yes, it is," he persisted; and he picked it up and gave it to her. Miss Phyllis smiled delightedly. Hilary had squeezed his wife's hand.

"Then we don't excuse it," said he.

I took out my watch. I was not finding much entertainment.

"Surely it's quite early, old man?" said Hilary.

"It's nearly eleven. We've spent half-an-hour on the thing," said I, peevishly, holding out my hand to my hostess.

"Oh, are you going? Good-night, Mr. Carter."

I turned to Miss Phyllis.

"I hope you won't think all love affairs are like that," I said; but I saw her lips begin to shape into "lovely," and I hastily left the room.

Hilary came to help me on with my coat.

He looked extremely apologetic, and very much ashamed of himself.

"Awfully sorry, old chap," said he, "that we bored you with our reminiscences. I know, of course, that they can't be very interesting to other people. Women are so confoundedly romantic."

"Don't try that on with me," said I, much disgusted. "You were just as bad yourself."

He laughed, as he leant against the door.

"She did look ripping in that white frock," he said, "with her hair —"

"Stop," said I, firmly. "She looked just like a lot of other girls."

"I'm hanged if she did!" said Hilary.

Then he glanced at me with a puzzled sort of expression.

"I say, old man, weren't you ever that way way yourself?" he asked.

I hailed a hansom cab.

"Because if you were, you know, you'd understand how a fellow remembers every —"

"Good-night," said I. "At least, I suppose you're not coming to the club?"

"Well, I think not," said Hilary. "Ta-ta, old fellow. Sorry we bored you. Of course, if a man has never —"

"Never!" I groaned. "A score of times!"

A VERY DULL AFFAIR

"Well, then, does n't it — ?"

"No," said I. "It's just that makes stories like yours so infernally — "

"What?" asked Hilary; for I had paused to light a cigarette.

"Uninteresting," said I, getting into my cab.

X
STRANGE, BUT TRUE

THE other day my young cousin George lunched with me. He is a cheery youth, and a member of the University of Oxford. He refreshes me very much, and I believe that I have the pleasure of affording him some matter for thought. On this occasion, however, he was extremely silent and depressed. I said little, but made an extremely good luncheon. Afterwards we proceeded to take a stroll in the Park.

"Sam, old boy," said George, suddenly, "I'm the most miserable devil alive."

"I don't know what else you expect at your age," I observed, lighting a cigar. He walked on in silence for a few moments.

"I say, Sam, old boy, when you were young, were you ever —?" He paused, arranged his neckcloth (it was more like a bed-quilt — oh, the fashion, of course, I know that), and blushed a fine crimson.

"Was I ever what, George?" I had the curiosity to ask.

STRANGE, BUT TRUE

"Oh, well, hard hit, you know — a girl, you know."

"In love, you mean, George? No, I never was."

"Never?"

"No. Are you?"

"Yes. Hang it!" Then he looked at me with a puzzled air and continued,—

"I say, though, Sam, it's awfully funny you shouldn't have — don't you know what it's like, then?"

"How should I?" I inquired apologetically. "What is it like, George?"

George took my arm.

"It's just Hades," he informed me confidentially.

"Then," I remarked, "I have no reason to regret — "

"Still, you know," interrupted George, "it's not half-bad."

"That appears to me to be a paradox," I observed.

"It's precious hard to explain it to you if you've never felt it," said George, in rather an injured tone. "But what I say is quite true."

"I shouldn't think of contradicting you, my dear fellow," I hastened to say.

"Let's sit down," said he, "and watch the people driving. We may see somebody — somebody we know, you know, Sam."

"So we may," said I, and we sat down.

"A fellow," pursued George, with knitted brows, "is all turned upside-down, don't you know?"

"How very peculiar!" I exclaimed.

"One moment he's the happiest dog in the world, and the next — well, the next, it's the deuce."

"But," I objected, "not surely without good reason for such a change?"

"Reason? Bosh! The least thing does it."

I flicked the ash from my cigar.

"It may," I remarked, "affect you in this extraordinary way, but surely it is not so with most people?"

"Perhaps not," George conceded. "Most people are cold-blooded asses."

"Very likely the explanation lies in that fact," said I.

"I didn't mean you, old chap," said George, with a penitence which showed that he had meant me.

"Oh, all right, all right," said I.

"But when a man's really far gone there's nothing else in the world but it."

"That seems to me not to be a healthy condition," said I.

"Healthy? Oh, you old idiot, Sam! Who's talking of health? Now, only last night I met her

STRANGE, BUT TRUE

at a dance. I had five dances with her—talked to her half the evening, in fact. Well, you'd think that would last some time, wouldn't you?"

"I should certainly have supposed so," I assented.

"So it would with most chaps, I dare say, but with me — confound it, I feel as if I hadn't seen her for six months!"

"But, my dear George, that is surely rather absurd! As you tell me, you spent a long while with the young person—"

"The — young — person!"

"You've not told me her name, you see."

"No, and I shan't. I wonder if she'll be at the Musgraves' to-night!"

"You're sure," said I, soothingly, "to meet her somewhere in the course of the next few weeks."

George looked at me. Then he observed with a bitter laugh,—

"It's pretty evident *you've* never had it. You're as bad as those chaps who write books."

"Well, but surely they often describe with sufficient warmth and — er — colour —"

"Oh, I dare say; but it's all wrong. At least, it's not what *I* feel. Then look at the girls in books! All *beasts!*"

George spoke with much vehemence; so that I was led to say,—

"The lady you are preoccupied with is, I suppose, handsome?"

George turned swiftly round on me.

"Look here, can you hold your tongue, Sam?"

I nodded.

"Then I'm hanged if I won't point her out to you!"

"That's uncommon good of you, George," said I.

"Then you'll see," continued George. "But it's not only her looks, you know, she's the most — "

He stopped. Looking round to see why, I observed that his face was red; he clutched his walking-stick tightly in his left hand; his right hand was trembling, as if it wanted to jump up to his hat. "Here she comes! Look, look!" he whispered.

Directing my eyes towards the lines of carriages which rolled past us, I observed a girl in a victoria; by her side sat a portly lady of middle age. The girl was decidedly like the lady; a description of the lady would not, I imagine, be interesting. The girl blushed slightly and bowed. George and I lifted our hats. The victoria and its occupants were gone. George leant back with a sigh. After a moment he said, —

"Well, that was her."

"*There is n't,*" said George, "*a girl in London to touch her*"

STRANGE, BUT TRUE

There was expectancy in his tone.

"She has an extremely prepossessing appearance," I observed.

"There is n't," said George, "a girl in London to touch her. Sam, old boy, I believe — I believe she likes me a bit."

"I 'm sure she must, George," said I; and, indeed, I thought so.

"The Governor 's infernally unreasonable," said George, fretfully.

"Oh, you 've mentioned it to him?"

"I sounded him. Oh, you may be sure he did n't see what I was up to. I put it quite generally. He talked rot about getting on in the world. Who wants to get on?"

"Who, indeed?" said I. "It is only changing what you are for something no better."

"And about waiting till I know my own mind. Is n't it enough to look at her?"

"Ample, in my opinion," said I.

George rose to his feet.

"They 've gone to a party; they won't come round again," said he. "We may as well go, may n't we?"

I was very comfortable; so I said timidly, —

"We might see somebody else we know."

"Oh, somebody else be hanged! Who wants to see 'em?"

THE DOLLY DIALOGUES

"I'm sure I don't," said I, hastily, as I rose from my armchair, which was at once snapped up.

We were about to return to the club, when I observed Lady Mickleham's barouche standing under the trees. I invited George to come and be introduced.

He displayed great indifference.

"She gives a good many parties," said I; "and perhaps —"

"By Jove! yes. I may as well," said George. "Glad you had the sense to think of that, old man."

So I took him up to Dolly and presented him. Dolly was very gracious : George is an eminently presentable boy. We fell into conversation.

"My cousin, Lady Mickleham," said I, "has been telling me —"

"Oh, shut up, Sam!" said George, not, however, appearing very angry.

"About a subject on which you can assist him more than I can, inasmuch as you are married. He is in love."

Dolly glanced at George.

"Oh, what fun!" said she.

"Fun!" cried George.

"I mean, how awfully interesting," said Dolly, suddenly transforming her expression.

"And he wanted to be introduced to you because you might ask her and him to —"

STRANGE, BUT TRUE

George became red, and began to stammer an apology.

"Oh, I don't believe him," said Dolly, kindly; "he always makes people uncomfortable if he can. What were you telling him, Mr. George?"

"It's no use telling him anything. He can't understand," said George.

"Is she very — ?" asked Dolly, fixing doubtfully grave eyes on my young cousin.

"Sam's seen her," said he, in an access of shyness.

Dolly turned to me for an opinion, and I gave one : —

"She is just," said I, "as charming as he thinks her."

Dolly leant over to my cousin, and whispered, "Tell me her name." And he whispered something back to Dolly.

"It's awfully kind of you, Lady Mickleham," he said.

"I am a kind old thing," said Dolly, all over dimples. "I can easily get to know them."

"Oh, you really are awfully kind, Lady Mickleham."

Dolly smiled upon him, waved her hand to me, and drove off, crying, —

"Do try to make Mr. Carter understand!"

We were left alone. George wore a meditative smile. Presently he roused himself to say, —

"She's really a very kind woman. She's so sympathetic. She's not like you. I expect she felt it once herself, you know."

"One can never tell," said I, carelessly. "Perhaps she did — once."

George fell to brooding again. I thought I would try an experiment.

"Not altogether bad-looking, either, is she?" I asked, lighting a cigarette.

George started.

"What? Oh, well, I don't know. I suppose some people might think so."

He paused, and added, with a bashful, knowing smile, —

"You can hardly expect *me* to go into raptures about her, can you, old man?"

I turned my head away, but he caught me.

"Oh, you needn't smile in that infernally patronising way," he cried angrily.

"Upon my word, George," said I, "I don't know that I need."

XI
THE VERY LATEST THING

"IT'S the very latest thing," said Lady Mickleham, standing by the table in the smoking-room, and holding an album in her hand.

"I wish it had been a little later still," said I, for I felt embarrassed.

"You promise, on your honour, to be absolutely sincere, you know, and then you write what you think of me. See what a lot of opinions I've got already," and she held up the thick album.

"It would be extremely interesting to read them," I observed.

"Oh! but they're quite confidential," said Dolly. "That's part of the fun."

"I don't appreciate that part," said I.

"Perhaps you will when you've written yours," suggested Lady Mickleham.

"Meanwhile, mayn't I see the Dowager's?"

"Well, I'll show you a little bit of the Dowager's. Look here: 'Our dear Dorothea is still perhaps just *a thought* wanting in seriousness, but the sense of her position is having a sobering effect.'"

"I hope not," I exclaimed apprehensively. "Whose is this?"

"Archie's."

"May I see a bit — ?"

"Not a bit," said Dolly. "Archie's is — is rather foolish, Mr. Carter."

"So I suppose," said I.

"Dear boy!" said Dolly, reflectively.

"I hate sentiment," said I. "Here's a long one. Who wrote — ?"

"Oh, you mustn't look at that — not at that, above all!"

"Why above all?" I asked with some severity.

Dolly smiled; then she observed in a soothing tone, —

"Perhaps it won't be 'above all' when you've written yours, Mr. Carter."

"By the way," I said carelessly, "I suppose Archie sees all of them?"

"He has never asked to see them," answered Lady Mickleham.

The reply seemed satisfactory; of course, Archie had only to ask. I took a clean quill and prepared to write.

"You promise to be sincere, you know," Dolly reminded me.

THE VERY LATEST THING

I laid down my pen.

"Impossible!" said I, firmly.

"Oh, but why, Mr. Carter?"

"There would be an end of our friendship."

"Do you think as badly of me as all that?" asked Dolly, with a rueful air.

I leant back in my chair and looked at Dolly. She looked at me. She smiled. I may have smiled.

"Yes," said I.

"Then you need n't write it *quite* all down," said Dolly.

"I am obliged," said I, taking up my pen.

"You must n't say what is n't true, but you need n't say everything that is — that might be — true," explained Dolly.

This, again, seemed satisfactory. I began to write, Dolly sitting opposite me with her elbows on the table, and watching me.

After ten minutes' steady work, which included several pauses for reflection, I threw down the pen, leant back in my chair, and lit a cigarette.

"Now read it," said Dolly, her chin in her hands and her eyes fixed on me.

"It is, on the whole," I observed, "complimentary."

"No, really?" said Dolly. "Yet you promised to be sincere."

THE DOLLY DIALOGUES

"You would not have had me disagreeable?" I asked.

"That's a different thing," said Dolly. "Read it, please."

"Lady Mickleham," I read, "is usually accounted a person of considerable attractions. She is widely popular, and more than one woman has been known to like her."

"I don't quite understand that," interrupted Dolly.

"It is surely simple," said I; and I read on without delay. "She is kind even to her husband, and takes the utmost pains to conceal from her mother-in-law anything calculated to distress that lady."

"I suppose you mean that to be nice?" said Dolly.

"Of course," I answered; and I proceeded: "She never gives pain to any one, except with the object of giving pleasure to somebody else, and her kindness is no less widely diffused than it is hearty and sincere."

"That really is nice," said Dolly, smiling.

"Thank you," said I, smiling also. "She is very charitable: she takes a pleasure in encouraging the shy and bashful —"

"How do *you* know that?" asked Dolly.

"While," I pursued, "suffering without impatience a considerable amount of self-assurance."

"*Lady Mickleham is usually accounted
a person of considerable attractions*"

THE VERY LATEST THING

"You can't know whether I'm patient or not," remarked Dolly. "I'm polite."

"She thinks," I read on, "no evil of the most attractive of women, and has a smile for the most unattractive of men."

"You put that very nicely," said Dolly, nodding.

"The former may constantly be seen in her house—and the latter at least as often as many people would think desirable." (Here for some reason Dolly laughed.) "Her intellectual powers are not despicable."

"Thank you, Mr. Carter."

"She can say what she means on the occasions on which she wishes to do so, and she is, at other times, equally capable of meaning much more than she would be likely to say."

"How do you mean that, Mr. Carter, please?"

"It explains itself," said I, and I proceeded: "The fact of her receiving a remark with disapprobation does not necessarily mean that it causes her displeasure, nor must it be assumed that she did not expect a visitor, merely on the ground that she greets him with surprise."

Here I observed Lady Mickleham looking at me rather suspiciously.

"I don't think that's *quite* nice of you, Mr. Carter," she said pathetically.

"Lady Mickleham is, in short," I went on,

coming to my peroration, " equally deserving of esteem and affection — "

" Esteem and affection ! That sounds just right," said Dolly, approvingly.

" And those who have been admitted to the enjoyment of her friendship are unanimous in discouraging all others from seeking a similar privilege."

" I beg your pardon ? " cried Lady Mickleham.

" Are unanimous," I repeated slowly and distinctly, " in discouraging all others from seeking a similar privilege."

Dolly looked at me, with her brow slightly puckered. I leant back, puffing at my cigarette. Presently — for there was quite a long pause — Dolly's lips curved.

" My mental powers are not despicable," she observed.

" I have said so," said I.

" I think I see," she remarked.

" Is there anything wrong ? " I asked anxiously.

" N-no," said Dolly, " not exactly wrong. In fact, I rather think I like that last bit best. Still, don't you think — ? "

She rose, came round the table, took up the pen, and put it back in my hand.

" What's this for ? " I asked.

" To correct the mistake," said Dolly.

THE VERY LATEST THING

"Do you really think so?" said I.

"I'm afraid so," said Dolly.

I took the pen and made a certain alteration. Dolly took up the album.

"'Are unanimous,'" she read, "'in encouraging all others to seek a similar privilege.' Yes, you meant that, you know, Mr. Carter."

"I suppose I must have," said I, rather sulkily.

"The other was nonsense," urged Dolly.

"Oh, utter nonsense," said I.

"And you had to write the truth!"

"Yes, I had to write some of it."

"And nonsense can't be the truth, can it, Mr. Carter?"

"Of course it can't, Lady Mickleham."

"Where are you going, Mr. Carter?" she asked; for I rose from my chair.

"To have a quiet smoke," said I.

"Alone?" asked Dolly.

"Yes, alone," said I.

I walked towards the door. Dolly stood by the table fingering the album. I had almost reached the door; then I happened to look round.

"Mr. Carter!" said Dolly, as though a new idea had struck her.

"What is it, Lady Mickleham?"

"Well, you know, Mr. Carter, I— I shall try to forget that mistake of yours."

"You're very kind, Lady Mickleham."

"But," said Dolly, with a troubled smile, "I — I'm quite afraid I shan't succeed, Mr. Carter."

After all, the smoking-room is meant for smoking.

XII

AN UNCOUNTED HOUR

WE were standing, Lady Mickleham and I, at a door which led from the morning-room to the terrace at The Towers. I was on a visit to that historic pile (by Vanbrugh — out of the money accumulated by the third Earl — Paymaster to the Forces — *temp.* Queen Anne). The morning-room is a large room. Archie was somewhere in it. Lady Mickleham held a jar containing *pâté de foie gras;* from time to time she dug a piece out with a fork and flung the morsel to a big retriever which was sitting on the terrace. The morning was fine but cloudy. Lady Mickleham wore blue. The dog swallowed the *pâté* with greediness.

"It's so bad for him," sighed she; "but the dear likes it so much."

"How human the creatures are!" said I.

"Do you know," pursued Lady Mickleham, "that the Dowager says I'm extravagant. She thinks dogs ought not to be fed on *pâté de foie gras.*"

THE DOLLY DIALOGUES

"Your extravagance," I observed, "is probably due to your having been brought up on a moderate income. I have felt the effect myself."

"Of course," said Dolly, "we are hit by the agricultural depression."

"The Carters also," I murmured, "are landed gentry."

"After all, I don't see much point in economy, do you, Mr. Carter?"

"Economy," I remarked, putting my hands in my pockets, "is going without something you do want in case you should, some day, want something which you probably won't want."

"Is n't that clever?" asked Dolly, in an apprehensive tone.

"Oh, dear, no," I answered reassuringly. "Anybody can do that — if they care to try, you know."

Dolly tossed a piece of *pâté* to the retriever.

"I have made a discovery lately," I observed.

"What are you two talking about?" called Archie.

"You're not meant to hear," said Dolly, without turning round.

"Yet if it's a discovery, he ought to hear it."

"He's made a good many lately," said Dolly.

She dug out the last bit of *pâté*, flung it to the dog, and handed the empty pot to me.

AN UNCOUNTED HOUR

"Don't be so allegorical," I implored. "Besides, it's really not just to Archie. No doubt the dog is a nice one, but —"

"How foolish you are this morning! What's the discovery?"

"An entirely surprising one."

"Oh, but let me hear! It's nothing about Archie, is it?"

"No. I've told you all Archie's sins."

"Nor Mrs. Hilary? I wish it was Mrs. Hilary!"

"Shall we walk on the terrace?" I suggested.

"Oh, yes, let's," said Dolly, stepping out, and putting on a broad-brimmed, low-crowned hat, which she caught up from a chair hard by. "It isn't Mrs. Hilary?" she added, sitting down on a garden seat.

"No," said I, leaning on a sun-dial which stood by the seat.

"Well, what is it?"

"It is simple," said I, "and serious. It is not, therefore, like you, Lady Mickleham."

"It's like Mrs. Hilary," said Dolly.

"No; because it isn't pleasant. By the way, are you jealous of Mrs. Hilary?"

Dolly said nothing at all. She took off her hat, roughened her hair a little, and assumed an effective pose. Still, it is a fact (for what it is worth) that she does n't care much about Mrs. Hilary.

"The discovery," I continued, "is that I 'm growing middle-aged."

"You are middle-aged," said Dolly, spearing her hat with its long pin.

I was, very naturally, nettled at this.

"So will you be soon," I retorted.

"Not soon," said Dolly.

"Some day," I insisted.

After a pause of about half a minute, Dolly said, "I suppose so."

"You will become," I pursued, idly drawing patterns with my finger on the sun-dial, "wrinkled, rough, fat — and, perhaps, good."

"You 're very disagreeable to-day," said Dolly.

She rose and stood by me.

"What do the mottoes mean?" she asked.

There were two: I will not say they contradicted one another, but they looked at life from different points of view.

"*Pereunt et imputantur*," I read.

"Well, what's that, Mr. Carter?"

"A trite, but offensive, assertion," said I, lighting a cigarette.

"But what does it mean?" she asked, a pucker on her forehead.

"What does it matter?" said I. "Let's try the other."

AN UNCOUNTED HOUR

"The other is longer."

"And better. *Horas non numero nisi serenas.*"

"And what's that?"

I translated literally. Dolly clapped her hands, and her face gleamed with smiles.

"I like that one!" she cried.

"Stop!" said I, imperatively. "You'll set it moving!"

"It's very sensible," said she.

"More freely rendered, it means, 'I live only when you—'"

"By Jove!" remarked Archie, coming up behind us, pipe in mouth, "there was a lot of rain last night. I've just measured it in the gauge."

"Some people measure everything," said I, with a displeased air. "It is a detestable habit."

"Archie, what does *Pereunt et imputantur* mean?"

"Eh? Oh, I see. Well, I say, Carter!—Oh, well, you know, I suppose it means you've got to pay for your fun, does n't it?"

"Oh, is that all? I was afraid it was something horrid. Why did you frighten me, Mr. Carter?"

"I think it is rather horrid," said I.

"Why, it is n't even true," said Dolly, scornfully.

Now when I heard this ancient and respectable legend thus cavalierly challenged I fell to studying it again, and presently I exclaimed,—

"Yes, you 're right! If it said that, it would n't be true; but Archie translated wrong."

"Well, you have a shot," suggested Archie.

"The oysters are eaten and put down in the bill," said I. "And you will observe, Archie, that it does not say in whose bill."

"Ah!" said Dolly.

"Well, somebody 's got to pay," persisted Archie.

"Oh, yes, somebody," laughed Dolly.

"Well, I don't know," said Archie. "I suppose the chap that has the fun —"

"It 's not always a chap," observed Dolly.

"Well, then, the individual," amended Archie. "I suppose he 'd have to pay."

"It does n't say so," I remarked mildly. "And according to my small experience —"

"I 'm quite sure your meaning is right, Mr. Carter," said Dolly, in an authoritative tone.

"As for the other motto, Archie," said I, "it merely means that a woman considers all hours wasted which she does not spend in the society of her husband."

"Oh, come, you don't gammon me," said Archie. "It means that the sun don't shine unless it 's fine, you know."

Archie delivered this remarkable discovery in a tone of great self-satisfaction.

AN UNCOUNTED HOUR

"Oh, you dear old thing!" said Dolly.

"Well, it does, you know," said he.

There was a pause. Archie kissed his wife (I am not complaining; he has, of course, a perfect right to kiss his wife) and strolled away towards the hot-houses.

I lit another cigarette. Then Dolly, pointing to the stem of the dial, cried, —

"Why, here's another inscription — oh, and in English!"

She was right. There was another — carelessly scratched on the old battered column — nearly effaced, for the characters had been but lightly marked — and yet not, as I conceived from the tenor of the words, very old.

"What is it?" asked Dolly, peering over my shoulder, as I bent down to read the letters, and shading her eyes with her hand. (Why didn't she put on her hat? We touch the Incomprehensible.)

"It is," said I, "a singularly poor, shallow, feeble, and undesirable little verse."

"Read it out," said Dolly.

So I read it. The silly fellow had written:

> "Life is Love, the poets tell us,
> In the little books they sell us;
> But pray, ma'am — what's of Life the Use,
> If Life be Love? For Love's the Deuce."

THE DOLLY DIALOGUES

Dolly began to laugh gently, digging the pin again into her hat.

"I wonder," said she, "whether they used to come and sit by this old dial just as we did this morning!"

"I shouldn't be at all surprised," said I. "And another point occurs to me, Lady Mickleham."

"Oh, does it? What's that, Mr. Carter?"

"Do you think that anybody measured the rain-gauge?"

Dolly looked at me very gravely.

"I'm so sorry when you do that," said she, pathetically.

I smiled.

"I really am," said Dolly. "But you don't mean it, do you?"

"Certainly not," said I.

Dolly smiled.

"No more than he did!" said I, pointing to the sun-dial.

And then we both smiled.

"Will this hour count, Mr. Carter?" asked Dolly, as she turned away.

"That would be rather strict," said I.

XIII

A REMINISCENCE

"I KNOW exactly what your mother wants, Phyllis," observed Mrs. Hilary.

"It's just to teach them the ordinary things," said little Miss Phyllis.

"What are the ordinary things?" I ventured to ask.

"What all girls are taught, of course, Mr. Carter," said Mrs. Hilary. "I'll write about it at once." And she looked at me as if she thought that I might be about to go.

"It is a comprehensive curriculum," I remarked, crossing my legs, "if one may judge from the results. How old are your younger sisters, Miss Phyllis?"

"Fourteen and sixteen," she answered.

"It is a pity," said I, "that this didn't happen a little while back. I knew a governess who would have suited the place to a 't.'"

Mrs. Hilary smiled scornfully.

"We used to meet," I continued.

"Who used to meet?" asked Miss Phyllis.

"The governess and myself, to be sure," said I, "under the old apple-tree in the garden at the back of the house."

"What house, Mr. Carter?"

"My father's house, of course, Miss Phyllis. And—"

"Oh, but that must be ages ago!" cried she.

Mrs. Hilary rose, cast one glance at me, and turned to the writing-table. Her pen began to scratch almost immediately.

"And under the apple-tree," I pursued, "we had many pleasant conversations."

"What about?" asked Miss Phyllis.

"One thing and another," I returned. "The schoolroom windows looked out that way,—a circumstance which made matters more comfortable for everybody."

"I should have thought—" began Miss Phyllis, smiling slightly, but keeping an apprehensive eye on Mrs. Hilary's back.

"Not at all," I interrupted. "My sisters saw us, you see. Well, of course they entertained an increased respect for me, which was all right, and a decreased respect for the governess, which was also all right. We met in the hour allotted to French lessons — by an undesigned but appropriate coincidence."

A REMINISCENCE

"I shall say about thirty-five, Phyllis," called Mrs. Hilary from the writing-table.

"Yes, Cousin Mary," called Miss Phyllis. "Did you meet often, Mr. Carter?"

"Every evening in the French hour," said I.

"She'll have got over any nonsense by then," called Mrs. Hilary. "They're often full of it."

"She had remarkably pretty hair," I continued; "very soft it was. Dear me! I was just twenty."

"How old was she?" asked Miss Phyllis.

"One's first love," said I, "is never any age. Everything went very well. Happiness was impossible. I was heart-broken, and the governess was far from happy. Ah, happy, happy times!"

"But you don't seem to have been happy," objected Miss Phyllis.

"Then came a terrible evening—"

"She ought to be a person of active habits," called Mrs. Hilary.

"I think so, yes, Cousin Mary. Oh, what happened, Mr. Carter?"

"And an early riser," added Mrs. Hilary.

"Yes, Cousin Mary. What *did* happen, Mr. Carter?"

"My mother came in during the French hour. I don't know whether you have observed, Miss Phyllis, how easy it is to slip into the habit of entering rooms when you had better remain outside. Now, even my friend Arch — However, that's neither here nor there. My mother, as I say, came in."

"Church of England, of course, Phyllis?" called Mrs. Hilary.

"Oh, of *course*, Cousin Mary," cried little Miss Phyllis.

"The sect makes no difference," I observed. "Well, my sisters, like good girls, began to repeat the irregular verbs. But it was no use. We were discovered. That night, Miss Phyllis, I nearly drowned myself."

"You must have been — Oh, how awful, Mr. Carter!"

"That is to say, I thought how effective it would be if I drowned myself. Ah, well, it could n't last!"

"And the governess?"

"She left next morning."

There was a pause. Miss Phyllis looked sad and thoughtful: I smiled pensively and beat my cane against my leg.

"Have you ever seen her since?" asked Miss Phyllis.

"No."

"Should n't — should n't you like to, Mr. Carter?"

A REMINISCENCE

"Heaven forbid!" said I.

Suddenly Mrs. Hilary pushed back her chair, and turned round to us.

"Well, I declare," said she, "I must be growing stupid. Here have I been writing to the Agency, when I know of the very thing myself! The Polwheedles' governess is just leaving them; she's been there over fifteen years. Lady Polwheedle told me she was a treasure. I wonder if she'd go!"

"Is she what mamma wants?"

"My dear, you'll be most lucky to get her. I'll write at once and ask her to come to lunch to-morrow. I met her there. She's an admirable person."

Mrs. Hilary wheeled round again. I shook my head at Miss Phyllis.

"Poor children!" said I. "Manage a bit of fun for them sometimes."

Miss Phyllis assumed a staid and virtuous air.

"They must be properly brought up, Mr. Carter," said she.

"Is there a House Opposite?" I asked; and Miss Phyllis blushed.

Mrs. Hilary advanced, holding out a letter.

"You may as well post this for me," said she. "Oh, and would you like to come to lunch to-morrow?"

THE DOLLY DIALOGUES

"To meet the Paragon?"

"No. She'll be there, of course; but you see it's Saturday, and Hilary will be here; and I thought you might take him off somewhere and leave Phyllis and me to have a quiet talk with her."

"That won't amuse her much," I ventured to remark.

"She's not coming to be *amused*," said Mrs. Hilary, severely.

"All right; I'll come," said I, taking my hat.

"Here's the note for Miss Bannerman," said Mrs. Hilary.

That sort of thing never surprises me. I looked at the letter and read "Miss M. E. Bannerman." "M. E." stood for "Maud Elizabeth." I put my hat back on the table.

"What sort of a looking person is this Miss Bannerman?" I asked.

"Oh, a spare, upright woman — hair a little gray, and — I don't know how to describe it — her face looks a little weather-beaten. She wears glasses."

"Thank you," said I. "And what sort of a looking person am I?"

Mrs. Hilary looked scornful. Miss Phyllis opened her eyes.

"How old do I look, Miss Phyllis?" I asked.

A REMINISCENCE

Miss Phyllis scanned me from top to toe.

"I don't know," she said uncomfortably.

"Guess," said I, sternly.

"F-forty-three — oh, or forty-two?" she asked, with a timid upward glance.

"When you 've done your nonsense — " began Mrs. Hilary; but I laid a hand on her arm.

"Should you call me fat?" I asked.

"Oh, no, not *fat*," said Mrs. Hilary, with a smile, which she strove to render reassuring.

"I am undoubtedly bald," I observed.

"You 're certainly bald," said Mrs. Hilary, with regretful candour.

I took my hat and remarked, —

"A man has a right to think of himself, but I am not thinking mainly of myself. I shall not come to lunch."

"You said you would," cried Mrs. Hilary, indignantly.

I poised the letter in my hand, reading again, "Miss M(aud) E(lizabeth) Bannerman." Miss Phyllis looked at me curiously, Mrs. Hilary impatiently.

"Who knows," said I, "that I may not be a Romance — a Vanished Dream — a Green Memory — an Oasis? A person who has the fortune to be an Oasis, Miss Phyllis, should be very careful. I will not come to lunch."

"Do you mean that you used to know Miss Bannerman?" asked Mrs. Hilary, in her pleasant prosaic way.

It was a sin seventeen years old: it would hardly count against the blameless Miss Bannerman now.

"You may tell her when I'm gone," said I to Miss Phyllis.

Miss Phyllis whispered in Mrs. Hilary's ear.

"Another!" cried Mrs. Hilary, aghast.

"It was the very first," said I, defending myself.

Mrs. Hilary began to laugh. I smoothed my hat.

"Tell her," said I, "that I remembered her very well."

"I shall do no such thing," said Mrs. Hilary.

"And tell her," I continued, "that I am still handsome."

"I shan't say a word about you," said Mrs. Hilary.

"Ah, well, that will be better still," said I.

"She'll have forgotten your very name," remarked Mrs. Hilary.

I opened the door, but a thought struck me. I turned round and observed,—

"I dare say her hair's just as soft as ever. Still — I'll lunch some other day."

XIV

ANCIENT HISTORY

"I'VE been hearing something about you, Mr. Carter," Dolly remarked, stroking the Persian kitten which she had bought to match her hair.

"I'm very weak. I shall like to hear it too." And I sat down.

Dolly kissed the kitten and went on. "About you and Dulcie Mildmay."

"That's very ancient history," said I, rather disgusted.

"You admit it is history, though?"

"History is what women have agreed to repeat, Lady Mickleham."

"Oh, if you're going to take it like that! I thought we were friends — and —"

"There is no greater mark of friendship," I observed, "than a complete absence of interest in one's doings."

"An absence of interest?" smiled Dolly, re-tying the kitten's bow in a meditative way.

"It makes the heart grow fonder (not, of course, that that's desirable). You notice, for example, that I don't ask where Archie is. It's not my business; it's enough for me that he isn't here."

"You always were easily pleased," said Dolly, kindly.

"So with you and me. When we are together, we are — "

"Friends," said she, with a touch of firmness, as I thought.

"We are, as I was about to say, happy. When I'm away, what am I to you? Nothing!"

"Well, I've an awful lot to do," murmured Dolly.

"And what are you to me?" I pursued. "A pleasing memory!"

"Thank you, Mr. Carter. But about Dulcie Mildmay?"

"Very well; only I wish you'd be a little more recent."

"You were in love with her, you know."

"I trust I'm always ready to learn," said I, resignedly.

"Oh, it's not as if I meant there was anything — anything there oughtn't to be."

"Then indeed we would discuss it."

"It was long before she married."

"*I've been hearing something about you, Mr. Carter*"

ANCIENT HISTORY

"You must really forgive me then. She married in — '94. April 15th, to be precise. I beg your pardon, Lady Mickleham?"

"I just smiled. You've such a splendid memory for dates."

"Uncle Joseph died last week and left me a legacy."

"It's really no use, Mr. Carter. Mrs. Hilary told me all about it."

"I never can conceal anything. It don't do, from Mrs. Hilary."

"You very nearly proposed to Dulcie, down the river one day. She had great difficulty in stopping you."

"Preposterous! Is there ever any difficulty in stopping me?"

Dolly placed the kitten on her left shoulder, so that it could rub its face against her ear. This action had all the effect of an observation.

"Though what you saw in her I can't think," she added.

"You should have asked me at the time," said I.

"Anyhow you were quite depressed for a month afterwards — Mrs. Hilary said so."

"Occasionally," I remarked, "Mrs. Hilary does me justice. I should have been depressed only —"

"Only what?"

"Thankfulness supervened," said I.

"Then you did nearly — ?"

"Oh, well, I was a little tempted, perhaps."

"You ought n't to yield to temptation."

"Well, somebody must, or the thing becomes absurd," said I.

"I shall have to keep my eye on you, Mr. Carter."

"Well, I like having pretty things about me—"

"That's rather obvious," interrupted Dolly, scornfully.

"And so," I pursued, "I daresay I enjoyed myself with Dulcie Mildmay."

Dolly put the kitten down on the floor with quite a bump. I took my hat.

"Your story," said I, as I brushed my hat, "has n't come to much, Lady Mickleham."

Dolly was not put out; nay, she picked up the kitten again and started rubbing its fur the wrong way.

"When you were a child, Mr. Carter —" she began.

"Dear, dear!" I murmured, stroking the crown of my head.

"Did you use to tell the truth?"

I put my hat back on the table. The conversation began to interest me.

"You may have noticed," said I, "that I am a man of method!"

ANCIENT HISTORY

"You do call regularly," Dolly agreed.

"I was the same at the B. C. sort of period you refer to. I had an invariable rule. I lied first."

"Yes, and then —?"

"Oh, they made a row. Then I told the truth, and was rewarded. If I'd told the truth the first time, you see, I should have got nothing. The thing would have degenerated into a matter of course, and I should have lost the benefit of confession."

"You got off, I suppose, by confessing?"

"I did. A halcyon period, Lady Mickleham. In later life one gets off by professing. Have you observed the difference?"

"Professing what?"

"An attachment to somebody else, to be sure. Weren't we talking of Dulcie Mildmay?"

"I asked you that question because Mrs. Hilary's little girl—"

"I am acquainted with that sad episode," I interposed. "Indeed, I took occasion to observe that I hoped it would make Mrs. Hilary more charitable to other people. As a matter of fact, it rather pleased me. Righteousness shouldn't run in families. It is all very well as a 'Sport,' but—"

"I don't see much sport in it," interrupted Dolly.

"I was speaking scientifically —"

"Then please don't." She paused and resumed in a thoughtful tone. "It reminded me of my first flirtation."

"This is indeed ancient history," I cried.

"Yes, I'm twenty-four."

In silent sympathy we stroked opposite ends of the Persian kitten.

"I didn't care one bit about him," Dolly assumed.

"Art for art's sake," said I, nodding approvingly.

"But there was nothing else to do and —"

"Are you busy this afternoon?"

"I was only sixteen and not very particular. I met him at the Wax-Works —"

"Are they so called because they make parents angry?"

"There was a hospital close to, and by an unlucky chance our Vicar induced mamma to visit it. Well, we ran into mamma coming out, you see."

"What happened?" I asked.

"Oh, I said I'd met him when I was with papa at Kissingen. Don't make another pun, please."

"Did papa play up?"

"I hadn't time to see him first," said Dolly, sadly. "Mamma drove down and picked him up in the City."

"I detest a suspicious temperament like that," said I. "What did it come to?"

ANCIENT HISTORY

"No parties, and extra French for weeks," sighed Dolly. "Mamma said she wouldn't have minded if only I'd spoken the truth."

"If she really meant that," I remarked cautiously, "there was the basis of an understanding."

"Of course she didn't. That was just rubbing it in, you know."

We relapsed into a pensive silence. Dolly gave the kitten milk, I pulled its tail. We had become quite thoughtful.

"I always tell the truth now, except to the Dowager," said Dolly, presently.

"It doesn't do to be quixotic," I agreed. "Telling the truth to people who misunderstand you is really promoting falsehood, isn't it?"

"That's rather a good idea," said Dolly. "And if you—"

"Adapt?"

"Yes—why then they get it just right, don't they? You think of quite sensible things sometimes, Mr. Carter."

"Often when I'm not with you," said I.

"And I suppose you adapted in telling me about Dulcie Mildmay?"

"Do you know, I've a sort of idea that I confused her with somebody else."

"That's not very complimentary."

"Oh, I don't know. I remember the scene so

well. It was in a backwater under a tree. There was a low bough over the water, and she —"

"Who?" asked Dolly, resuming exclusive possession of the kitten.

"Well, whoever it was — hung her hat on the bough. It was about eight o'clock, a very pleasant evening. I happen to recollect that the cushions were blue. And she wore blue. And I was blue, until — Did you say that she refused me?"

"Mrs. Hilary says she did n't let it come to that."

"Mrs. Hilary is right as usual. We got home at ten and — Your mother could n't have meant what she said, I think."

"I don't see how mamma comes in," said Dolly, in a voice muffled by kitten fur.

"Because her mother minded considerably, although we spoke the truth."

"What did you do that for?" asked Dolly, reprovingly.

"Oh, because other people had seen us from a punt. So we just said that time had flown — not, perhaps, a particularly tactful thing to say. And that's the whole truth about Dulcie Mildmay."

I rose and took my hat again, as if I meant it this time too. Dolly rose too, and held out one hand to me; the other contained the kitten.

ANCIENT HISTORY

"What was the hat like?" asked Dolly.

"Just such a hat as you'd wear yourself," said I.

"I never wear hats like Dulcie Mildmay's."

"I told you there was a mistake somewhere," I observed triumphantly.

Dolly smiled; she looked up at me (well, I'm taller than she is, of course).

"Yes, I expect there is," said she. "But do you see any particular good in telling Mrs. Hilary so?"

"She would n't believe it."

"No — and — "

"It is, as you observe, so uncomplimentary to Mrs. Mildmay."

"And it's all such very Ancient History!"

I don't think anything more of interest occurred that afternoon — anyhow nothing more about Dulcie Mildmay.

XV

A FINE DAY

"I SEE nothing whatever to laugh at," said Mrs. Hilary, coldly, when I had finished.

"I did not ask you to laugh," I observed mildly. "I mentioned it merely as a typical case."

"It's not typical," she said, and took up her embroidery. But a moment later she added,—

"Poor boy! I'm not surprised!"

"I'm not surprised either," I remarked. "It is, however, extremely deplorable."

"It's your own fault. Why did you introduce him?"

"A book," I observed, "might be written on the Injustice of the Just. How could I suppose that he would—?"

By the way, I may as well state what he— that is, my young cousin George— had done. Unless one is a genius, it is best to aim at being intelligible.

Well, he was in love; and with a view of providing him with another house at which he might

A FINE DAY

be likely to meet the adored object, I presented him to my friend Lady Mickleham. That was on a Tuesday. A fortnight later, as I was sitting in Hyde Park (as I sometimes do), George came up and took the chair next to me. I gave him a cigarette, but made no remark. George beat his cane restlessly against the leg of his trousers.

"I've got to go up to-morrow," he remarked.

"Ah, well, Oxford is a delightful town," said I.

"D—d hole," observed George.

I was about to contest this opinion when a victoria drove by.

A girl sat in it, side by side with a portly lady.

"George, George!" I cried. "There she is — Look!"

George looked, raised his hat with sufficient politeness, and remarked to me, —

"Hang it! one sees those people everywhere."

I am not easily surprised, but I confess I turned to George with an expression of wonder.

"A fortnight ago — " I began.

"Don't be an ass, Sam," said George, rather sharply. "She's not a bad girl, but — " He broke off and began to whistle.

There was a long pause. I lit a cigar, and looked at the people.

THE DOLLY DIALOGUES

"I lunched at the Micklehams' to-day," said George, drawing a figure on the gravel with his cane. "Mickleham's not a bad fellow."

"One of the best fellows alive," I agreed.

"I wonder why she married him, though," mused George; and he added, with apparent irrelevance, "It's a dashed bore, going up." And then a smile spread over his face; a blush accompanied it, and proclaimed George's sense of delicious wickedness. I turned on him.

"Out with it!" said I.

"It's nothing. Don't be a fool," said George.

"Where did you get that rose?" I asked.

"This rose?" he repeated, fondling the blossom. "It was given to me."

Upon this I groaned — and I still consider that I had good reason for my action. It was the groan of a moralist.

"They've asked me to stay at The Towers next vac.," said George, glancing at me out of the corner of an immoral eye. Perhaps he thought it too immoral, for he added, "It's all *right*, Sam." I believe that I have as much self-control as most people, but at this point I chuckled.

"What the deuce are you laughing at?" asked George.

I made no answer, and he went on, —

"You never told me what a — what she was

A FINE DAY

like, Sam. Wanted to keep it to yourself, you old dog."

"George — George — George!" said I. "You go up to-morrow?"

"Yes, confound it!"

"And term lasts two months?"

"Yes — hang it!"

"All is well," said I, crossing my legs. "There is more virtue in two months than in Ten Commandments."

George regarded me with a dispassionate air.

"You're an awful ass sometimes," he observed critically, and he rose from his seat.

"Must you go?" said I.

"Yes — got a lot of things to do. Look here, Sam, don't go and talk about — "

"Talk about what?"

"Anything, you old idiot," said George, with a pleased smile, and he dug me in the ribs with his cane, and departed.

I sat on, admiring the simple elements which constitute the happiness of the young. Alas! with advancing years, Wrong loses half its flavour! To be improper ceases, by itself, to satisfy.

Immersed in these reflections, I failed to notice that a barouche had stopped opposite to me; and suddenly I found a footman addressing me.

"Beg your pardon, sir," he said. "Her ladyship wishes to speak to you."

"It is a blessed thing to be young, Martin," I observed.

"Yes, sir," said Martin. "It's a fine day, sir."

"But very short," said I. Martin is respectful, and said nothing — to me, at least. What he said to the coachman, I don't know.

And then I went up to Dolly.

"Get in and drive round," suggested Dolly.

"I can't," said I. "I have a bad nose."

"What's the matter with your nose?" asked Dolly, smiling.

"The joint is injured," said I, getting into the barouche. And I added severely, "I suppose I'd better sit with my back to the horses?"

"Oh, no, you're not my husband," said Dolly. "Sit here;" and she made room by her, as she continued, "I rather like Mr. George."

"I'm ashamed of you," I observed. "Considering your age — "

"Mr. Carter!"

"Considering, I say, his age, your conduct is scandalous. I shall never introduce any nice boys to you again."

"Oh, please do," said Dolly, clasping her hands.

"You give them roses," said I, accusingly. "You make them false to their earliest loves — "

"He's a nice boy," said she. "How like he is to you, Mr. Carter"

A FINE DAY

"She was a pudding-faced thing," observed Dolly.

I frowned. Dolly, by an accident, allowed the tip of her finger to touch my arm for an instant.

"He's a nice boy," said she. "How like he is to you, Mr. Carter!"

"I am a long way past that," said I. "I am thirty-six."

"If you mean to be disagreeable!" said she, turning away. "I beg your pardon for touching you, Mr. Carter."

"I did not notice it, Lady Mickleham."

"Would you like to get out?"

"It's miles from my club," said I, discontentedly.

"He's such fun," said Dolly, with a sudden smile. "He told Archie that I was the most charming woman in London! You've never done that!"

"He said the same about the pudding-faced girl," I observed.

There was a pause. Then Dolly asked,—

"How is your nose?"

"The carriage-exercise is doing it good," said I.

"If," observed Dolly, "he is so silly now, what will he be at your age?"

"A wise man," said I.

"He suggested that I might write to him," bubbled Dolly.

THE DOLLY DIALOGUES

Now when Dolly bubbles — an operation which includes a sudden turn towards me, a dancing of eyes, a dart of a small hand, a hurried rush of words, checked and confused by a speedier gust of gurgling sound — I am in the habit of ceasing to argue the question. Bubbling is not to be met by arguing. I could only say, —

"He'll have forgotten by the end of the term."

"He'll remember two days later," retorted Dolly.

"Stop the carriage," said I. "I shall tell Mrs. Hilary all about it."

"I won't stop the carriage," said Dolly. "I'm going to take you home with me."

"I am at a premium to-day," I said sardonically.

"One must have something," said Dolly. "How is your nose now, Mr. Carter?"

I looked at Dolly. I had better not have done that.

"Would afternoon tea hurt it?" she inquired anxiously.

"It would do it good," said I, decisively.

And that is absolutely the whole story. And what in the world Mrs. Hilary found to disapprove of I don't know — especially as I did n't tell her half of it! But she did disapprove. However, she looks very well when she disapproves.

XVI

THE HOUSE OPPOSITE

WE were talking over the sad case of young Algy Groom; I was explaining to Mrs. Hilary exactly what had happened.

"His father gave him," said I, "a hundred pounds, to keep him for three months in Paris while he learnt French."

"And very liberal too," said Mrs. Hilary.

"It depends where you dine," said I. "However, that question did not arise, for Algy went to the Grand Prix the day after he arrived—"

"A *horse race?*" asked Mrs. Hilary, with great contempt.

"Certainly the competitors are horses," I rejoined. "And there he, most unfortunately, lost the whole sum, without learning any French to speak of."

"How disgusting!" exclaimed Mrs. Hilary, and little Miss Phyllis gasped in horror.

"Oh, well," said Hilary, with much bravery (as it struck me), "his father's very well off."

THE DOLLY DIALOGUES

"That doesn't make it a bit better," declared his wife.

"There's no mortal sin in a little betting, my dear. Boys will be boys —"

"And even that," I interposed, "wouldn't matter if we could only prevent girls from being girls."

Mrs. Hilary, taking no notice whatever of me, pronounced sentence. "He grossly deceived his father," she said, and took up her embroidery.

"Most of us have grossly deceived our parents before now," said I. "We should all have to confess to something of the sort."

"I hope you're speaking for your own sex," observed Mrs. Hilary.

"Not more than yours," said I. "You used to meet Hilary on the pier when your father wasn't there — you told me so."

"Father had authorised my acquaintance with Hilary."

"I hate quibbles," said I.

There was a pause. Mrs. Hilary stitched: Hilary observed that the day was fine.

"Now," I pursued carelessly, "even Miss Phyllis here has been known to deceive her parents."

"Oh, let the poor child alone, anyhow," said Mrs. Hilary.

"Haven't you?" said I to Miss Phyllis.

THE HOUSE OPPOSITE

I expected an indignant denial. So did Mrs. Hilary, for she remarked with a sympathetic air, —

"Never mind his folly, Phyllis dear."

"Have n't you, Miss Phyllis?" said I.

Miss Phyllis grew very red. Fearing that I was causing her pain, I was about to observe on the prospects of a Dissolution when a shy smile spread over Miss Phyllis's face.

"Yes, once," said she, with a timid glance at Mrs. Hilary, who immediately laid down her embroidery.

"Out with it," I cried triumphantly. "Come along, Miss Phyllis. We won't tell, honour bright!"

Miss Phyllis looked again at Mrs. Hilary. Mrs. Hilary is human.

"Well, Phyllis dear," said she, "after all this time I should n't think it my duty —"

"It only happened last summer," said Miss Phyllis.

Mrs. Hilary looked rather put out.

"Still," she began.

"We must have the story," said I.

Little Miss Phyllis put down the sock she had been knitting.

"I was very naughty," she remarked. "It was my last term at school."

"I know that age," said I to Hilary.

"My window looked out towards the street. You're sure you won't tell? Well, there was a house opposite —"

"And a young man in it," said I.

"How did you know that?" asked Miss Phyllis, blushing immensely.

"No girls' school can keep up its numbers without one," I explained.

"Well, there was, anyhow," said Miss Phyllis. "And I and two other girls went to a course of lectures at the Town Hall on literature or something of that kind. We used to have a shilling given us for our tickets."

"Precisely," said I. "A hundred pounds!"

"No, a shilling," corrected Miss Phyllis. "A hundred pounds! How absurd, Mr. Carter! Well, one day I — I —"

"You're sure you wish to go on, Phyllis?" asked Mrs. Hilary.

"You're afraid, Mrs. Hilary," said I, severely.

"Nonsense, Mr. Carter. I thought Phyllis might —"

"I don't mind going on," said Miss Phyllis, smiling. "One day I — I lost the other girls."

"The other girls are always easy to lose," I observed.

"And on the way there, — oh, you know, he went to the lectures."

THE HOUSE OPPOSITE

"The young dog," said I, nudging Hilary. "I should think he did!"

"On the way there it became rather — rather foggy."

"Blessings on it!" I cried; for little Miss Phyllis's demure but roguish expression delighted me.

"And he — he found me in the fog."

"What are you doing, Mr. Carter?" cried Mrs. Hilary, angrily.

"Nothing, nothing," said I. I believe I had winked at Hilary.

"And — and we couldn't find the Town Hall."

"Oh, Phyllis!" groaned Mrs. Hilary.

Little Miss Phyllis looked alarmed for a moment. Then she smiled.

"But we found the confectioner's," said she.

"The *Grand Prix*," said I, pointing my forefinger at Hilary.

"He had no money at all," said Miss Phyllis.

"It's ideal!" said I.

"And — and we had tea on — on —"

"The shilling?" I cried in rapture.

"Yes," said little Miss Phyllis, "on the shilling. And he saw me home."

"Details, please," said I.

Little Miss Phyllis shook her head.

"And left me at the door."

"Was it still foggy?" I asked.

"Yes. Or he wouldn't have—"

"Now what did he—?"

"Come to the door, Mr. Carter," said Miss Phyllis, with obvious wariness. "Oh, it was such fun!"

"I'm sure it was."

"No, I mean when we were examined in the lectures. I bought the local paper, you know, and read it up, and I got top marks easily, and Miss Green wrote to mother to say how well I had done."

"It all ends most satisfactorily," I observed.

"Yes, didn't it?" said little Miss Phyllis.

Mrs. Hilary was grave again.

"And you never told your mother, Phyllis!" she asked.

"N-no, Cousin Mary," said Miss Phyllis.

I rose and stood with my back to the fire. Little Miss Phyllis took up her sock again, but a smile still played about the corners of her mouth.

"I wonder," said I, looking up at the ceiling, "what happened at the door." Then, as no one spoke, I added,—

"Pooh! I know what happened at the door."

"I'm not going to tell you anything more," said Miss Phyllis.

THE HOUSE OPPOSITE

"But I should like to hear it in your own —"

Miss Phyllis was gone! She had suddenly risen and run from the room.

"It did happen at the door," said I.

"Fancy Phyllis!" mused Mrs. Hilary.

"I hope," said I, "that it will be a lesson to you."

"I shall have to keep my eye on her," said Mrs. Hilary.

"You can't do it," said I, in easy confidence. I had no fear of little Miss Phyllis being done out of her recreations. "Meanwhile," I pursued, "the important thing is this: my parallel is obvious and complete."

"There's not the least likeness," said Mrs. Hilary, sharply.

"As a hundred pounds are to a shilling, so is the Grand Prix to the young man opposite," I observed, taking my hat, and holding out my hand to Mrs. Hilary.

"I am very angry with you," she said. "You've made the child think there was nothing wrong in it."

"Oh! nonsense," said I. "Look how she enjoyed telling it."

Then, not heeding Mrs. Hilary, I launched into an apostrophe.

"O divine House Opposite!" I cried. "Charming House Opposite! What is a man's own dull uneventful home compared with that Glorious House Opposite! If only I might dwell for ever in the House Opposite!"

"I haven't the least notion what you mean," remarked Mrs. Hilary, stiffly. "I suppose it's something silly — or worse."

I looked at her in some puzzle.

"Have you no longing for the House Opposite?" I asked.

Mrs. Hilary looked at me. Her eyes ceased to be absolutely blank. She put her arm through Hilary's and answered gently, —

"I don't want the House Opposite."

"Ah," said I, giving my hat a brush, "but maybe you remember the House — when it was Opposite?"

Mrs. Hilary, one arm still in Hilary's gave me her hand.

She blushed and smiled.

"Well," said she, "it was your fault: so I won't scold Phyllis."

"No, don't, my dear," said Hilary, with a laugh.

As for me, I went downstairs, and, in absence of mind, bade my cabman drive to the House Opposite. But I have never got there.

XVII

A QUICK CHANGE

"WHY not go with Archie?" I asked, spreading out my hands.

"It will be dull enough, anyhow," said Dolly, fretfully. "Besides, it's awfully *bourgeois* to go to the theatre with one's husband."

"*Bourgeois*," I observed, "is an epithet which the riff-raff apply to what is respectable, and the aristocracy to what is decent."

"But it's not a nice thing to be, all the same," said Dolly, who is impervious to the most penetrating remark.

"You're in no danger of it," I hastened to assure her.

"How should you describe me, then?" she asked, leaning forward, with a smile.

"I should describe you, Lady Mickleham," I replied discreetly, "as being a little lower than the angels."

Dolly's smile was almost a laugh as she asked.

"How much lower, please, Mr. Carter?"

"Just by the depth of your dimples," said I, thoughtlessly.

Dolly became immensely grave.

"I thought," said she, "that we never mentioned them now, Mr. Carter."

"Did we ever?" I asked innocently.

"I seemed to remember once: do you recollect being in very low spirits one evening at Monte?"

"I remember being in very low water more than one evening there."

"Yes: you told me you were terribly hard up."

"There was an election in our division that year," I remarked, "and I remitted thirty per cent of my rents."

"You did — to M. Blanc," said Dolly. "Oh, and you were very dreary! You said you'd wasted your life and your time and your opportunities."

"Oh, you mustn't suppose I never have any proper feelings," said I, complacently.

"I think you were hardly yourself."

"Do be more charitable."

"And you said that your only chance was in gaining the affection of—"

"Surely I was not such an — so foolish?" I implored.

"Yes, you were. You were sitting close by me—"

"Oh, then, it doesn't count," said I, rallying a little.

"On a bench. You remember the bench?"

"*You were sitting close by me — on a bench*"

A QUICK CHANGE

"No, I don't," said I, with a kind but firm smile.

"Not the bench?"

"No."

Dolly looked at me, then she asked in an insinuating tone, —

"When did you forget it, Mr. Carter?"

"The day you were buried," I rejoined.

"I see. Well, you said then what you could n't possibly have meant."

"I dare say. I often did."

"That they were — "

"That what were?"

"Why, the — the — what we 're talking about."

"What we were — ? Oh, to be sure, the — the blemishes?"

"Yes, the blemishes. You said they were the most — "

"Oh, well, it was a *façon de parler*."

"I was afraid you were n't a bit sincere," said Dolly, humbly.

"Well, judge me by yourself," said I, with a candid air.

"But I said nothing!" cried Dolly.

"It was incomparably the most artistic thing to do," said I.

"I 'm sometimes afraid you don't do me justice, Mr. Carter," remarked Dolly, with some pathos.

I did not care to enter upon that discussion, and a pause followed. Then Dolly, in a timid manner, asked me, —

"Do you remember the dreadful thing that happened the same evening?"

"That chances to remain in my memory," I admitted.

"I've always thought it kind of you never to speak of it," said she.

"It is best forgotten," said I, smiling.

"We should have said the same about anybody," protested Dolly.

"Certainly. We were only trying to be smart," said I.

"And it was horribly unjust."

"I quite agree with you, Lady Mickleham."

"Besides, I didn't know anything about him then. He had only arrived that day, you see."

"Really we were not to blame," I urged.

"Oh, but doesn't it seem funny?"

"A strange whirligig, no doubt," I mused.

There was a pause. Then the faintest of smiles appeared on Dolly's face.

"He shouldn't have worn such clothes," she said, as though in self-defence. "Anybody would have looked absurd in them."

"It was all the clothes," I agreed. "Besides,

A QUICK CHANGE

when a man does n't know a place, he always moons about and looks—"

"Yes. Rather awkward, does n't he, Mr. Carter?"

"And the mere fact of his looking at you—"

"At us, please."

"Is nothing, although we made a grievance of it at the time."

"That was very absurd of you," said Dolly.

"It was certainly unreasonable of us," said I.

"We ought to have known he was a gentleman."

"But we scouted the idea of it," said I.

"It was a most curious mistake to make," said Dolly.

"Oh, well, it's all put right now," said I.

"Oh, Mr. Carter, do you remember mamma's face when we described him?"

"That was a terrible moment," said I, with a shudder.

"I said he was — ugly," whispered Dolly.

"And I said — something worse," murmured I.

"And mamma knew at once from our description that it was —"

"She saw it in a minute," said I.

"And then you went away."

"Well, I rather suppose I did," said I.

"Mamma is just a little like the Dowager sometimes," said Dolly.

"There is a touch now and then," I conceded.

"And when I was introduced to him the next day I absolutely blushed."

"I don't altogether wonder at that," I observed.

"But it wasn't as if he'd heard what we were saying."

"No; but he'd seen what we were doing."

"Well, what were we doing?" cried Dolly, defiantly.

"Conversing confidentially," said I.

"And a week later you went home!"

"Just one week later," said I.

There was a long pause.

"Well, you'll take me to the theatre?" asked Dolly, with something which, if I were so disposed, I might consider a sigh.

"I've seen the piece twice," said I.

"How tiresome of you! You've seen everything twice."

"I've seen some things much oftener," I observed.

"I'll get a nice girl for you to talk to, and I'll have a young man."

"I don't want my girl to be too *nice*," I observed.

"She shall be pretty," said Dolly, generously.

"I don't mind if I do come with you," said I. "What becomes of Archie?"

A QUICK CHANGE

"He's going to take his mother and sisters to the Albert Hall."

My face brightened.

"I am unreasonable," I admitted.

"Sometimes you are," said Dolly.

"I have much to be thankful for. Have you ever observed a small boy eat a penny ice?"

"Of course I have," said Dolly.

"What does he do when he's finished it?"

"Stops, I suppose."

"On the contrary," said I, "he licks the glass."

"Yes, he does," said Dolly, meditatively.

"It's not so bad, — licking the glass," said I.

Dolly stood opposite me, smiling. At this moment Archie entered. He had been working at his lathe. He is very fond of making things which he does n't want, and then giving them to people who have no use for them.

"How are you, old chap?" he began. "I've just finished an uncommon pretty — "

He stopped, paralysed by a cry from Dolly, —

"Archie, what in the world are you wearing?"

I turned a startled gaze upon Archie.

"It's just an old suit I routed out," said he, apologetically.

I looked at Dolly; her eyes were close shut, and she gasped, —

"My dear, dear boy, go and change it!"

" I don't see why it's not — "

" Go and change it, if you love me," besought Dolly.

" Oh, all right."

" You look hideous in it," she said, her eyes still shut.

Archie, who is very docile, withdrew. A guilty silence reigned for some moments. Then Dolly opened her eyes.

" It was the suit," she said, with a shudder. " Oh, how it all came back to me! "

" I could wish," I observed, taking my hat, " that it would all come back to me."

" I wonder if you mean that! "

" As much as I ever did," said I, earnestly.

" And that is — ? "

" Quite enough."

" How tiresome you are! " she said, turning away with a smile.

Outside I met Archie in another suit.

" A quick change, eh, my boy? " said he.

" It took just a week," I remarked absently.

Archie stared.

XVIII

A SLIGHT MISTAKE

"I DON'T ask you for more than a guinea," said Mrs. Hilary, with a parade of forbearance.

"It would be the same," I replied politely, "if you asked me for a thousand;" with which I handed her half-a-crown. She held it in her open hand, regarding it scornfully.

"Yes," I continued, taking a seat, "I feel that pecuniary gifts — "

"Half-a-crown!"

"Are a poor substitute for personal service. May not I accompany you to the ceremony?"

"I dare say you spent as much as this on wine with your lunch!"

"I was in a mad mood to-day," I answered apologetically. "What are they taught at the school?"

"Above all, to be good girls," said Mrs. Hilary, earnestly. "What are you sneering at, Mr. Carter?"

"Nothing," said I, hastily, and I added with a sigh, "I suppose it's all right."

"I should like," said Mrs. Hilary, meditatively, "if I had not other duties, to dedicate my life to the service of girls."

"I should think twice about that, if I were you," said I, shaking my head.

"By the way, Mr. Carter, I don't know if I've ever spoken unkindly of Lady Mickleham. I hope not."

"Hope," said I, "is not yet taxed."

"If I have, I'm very sorry. She's been most kind in undertaking to give away the prizes to-day. There must be some good in her."

"Oh, don't be hasty!" I implored.

"I always *wanted* to think well of her."

"Ah! Now I never did."

"And Lord Mickleham is coming, too. He'll be most useful."

"That settles it," I exclaimed. "I may not be an earl, but I have a perfect right to be useful. I'll go too."

"I wonder if you'll behave properly," said Mrs. Hilary, doubtfully.

I held out a half-sovereign, three half-crowns, and a shilling.

"Oh, well, you may come, since Hilary can't," said Mrs. Hilary.

A SLIGHT MISTAKE

"You mean he won't," I observed.

"He has always been prevented hitherto," said she, with dignity.

So I went, and it proved a most agreeable expedition. There were two hundred girls in blue frocks and white aprons (the girl three from the end of the fifth row was decidedly pretty) — a nice lot of prize books — the Micklehams (Dolly in demure black), ourselves, and the matron. All went well. Dolly gave away the prizes; Mrs. Hilary and Archie made little speeches. Then the matron came to me. I was sitting modestly at the back of the platform, a little distance behind the others.

"Mr. Musgrave," said the matron to me, "we're so glad to see you here at last. Won't you say a few words?"

"It would be a privilege," I responded cordially, "but unhappily I have a sore throat."

The matron (who was a most respectable woman) said, "Dear, dear!" but did not press the point. Evidently, however, she liked me, for when we went to have a cup of tea, she got me in a corner and began to tell me all about the work. It was extremely interesting. Then the matron observed, —

"And what an angel Mrs. Musgrave is!"

"Well, I should hardly call her that," said I, with a smile.

"Oh, you must n't depreciate her,— you, of all men!" cried the matron, with a somewhat ponderous archness. "Really I envy you her constant society."

"I assure you," said I, "I see very little of her."

"I beg your pardon?"

"I only go to the house about once a fortnight — Oh, it's not my fault. She won't have me there oftener."

"What do you mean? I beg your pardon. Perhaps I've touched on a painful —?"

"Not at all, not at all," said I, suavely. "It is very natural. I am neither young nor handsome, Mrs. Wiggins. I am not complaining."

The matron gazed at me.

"Only seeing her here," I pursued, "you have no idea of what she is at home. She has chosen to forbid me to come to her house —"

"Her house?"

"It happens to be more hers than mine," I explained. "To forbid me, I say, more than once to come to her house. No doubt she had her reasons."

"Nothing could justify it," said the matron, directing a wondering glance at Mrs. Hilary.

"Do not let us blame her," said I. "It is just an unfortunate accident. She is not as fond of me

A SLIGHT MISTAKE

as I could wish, Mrs. Wiggins; and she is a great deal fonder than I could wish of—"

I broke off. Mrs. Hilary was walking towards us. I think she was pleased to see me getting on so well with the matron, for she was smiling pleasantly. The matron wore a bewildered expression.

"I suppose," said Mrs. Hilary, "that you'll drive back with the Micklehams?"

"Unless you want me," said I, keeping a watchful eye on the matron.

"Oh, I don't want you," said Mrs. Hilary, lightly.

"You won't be alone this evening?" I asked anxiously.

Mrs. Hilary stared a little.

"Oh, no!" she said. "We shall have our usual party."

"May I come one day next week?" I asked humbly.

Mrs. Hilary thought for a moment.

"I'm so busy next week; come the week after," said she, giving me her hand.

"That's very unkind," said I.

"Nonsense!" said Mrs. Hilary, and she added, "Mind you let me know when you're coming."

"I won't surprise you," I assured her, with a covert glance at the matron.

THE DOLLY DIALOGUES

The excellent woman was quite red in the face, and could gasp out nothing but "Good-by," as Mrs. Hilary affectionately pressed her hand.

At this moment Dolly came up. She was alone.

"Where's Archie?" I asked.

"He's run away; he's got to meet somebody. I knew you'd see me home. Mrs. Hilary didn't want you, of course?"

"Of course not," said I, plaintively.

"Besides, you'd rather come with me, wouldn't you?" pursued Dolly, and she added pleasantly to the matron, "Mrs. Hilary's so down on him, you know."

"I'd much rather come with you," said I.

"We'll have a cosy drive all to ourselves," said Dolly, "without husbands or wives or anything horrid. Isn't it nice to get rid of one's husband sometimes, Mrs. Wiggins?"

"I have the misfortune to be a widow, Lady Mickleham," said Mrs. Wiggins.

Dolly's eye rested upon her with an interested expression. I knew that she was about to ask Mrs. Wiggins whether she liked the condition of life, and I interposed hastily, with a sigh, —

"But *you* can look back on a happy marriage, Mrs. Wiggins?"

"I did my best to make it so," said she, stiffly.

A SLIGHT MISTAKE

"You're right," said I. "Even in the face of unkindness we should strive —"

"My husband's not unkind," said Dolly.

"I did n't mean your husband," said I.

"What your poor wife would do if she cared a button for you, I don't know," observed Dolly.

"If I had a wife who cared for me, I should be a better man," said I, solemnly.

"But you 'd probably be very dull," said Dolly. "And you would n't be allowed to drive with me."

"Perhaps it's all for the best," said I, brightening up. "*Good*-by, Mrs. Wiggins."

Dolly walked on. Mrs. Wiggins held my hand for a moment.

"Young man," said she, sternly, "are you sure it's not your own fault?"

"I'm not at all sure, Mrs. Wiggins," said I. "But don't be distressed about it. It's of no consequence. I don't let it make me unhappy. Good-by; so many thanks. Charming girls you have here — especially that one in the fifth — I mean, charming, all of them. Good-by."

I hastened to the carriage. Mrs. Wiggins stood and watched. I got in and sat down by Dolly.

"Oh, Mrs. Wiggins," said Dolly, dimpling, "don't tell Mrs. Hilary that Archie was n't with us, or we shall get into trouble." And she added to me, "Are you all right?"

"Rather!" said I, appreciatively; and we drove off, leaving Mrs. Wiggins on the door-step.

A fortnight later I went to call on Mrs. Hilary. After some conversation she remarked, —

"I'm going to the school again to-morrow."

"Really!" said I.

"And I'm so delighted — I've persuaded Hilary to come."

She paused, and then added, —

"You really seemed interested last time."

"Oh, I was."

"Would you like to come again to-morrow?"

"No, I think not, thanks," said I, carelessly.

"That's just like you!" she said severely. "You never do any real good, because you never stick to anything."

"There are some things one can't stick to," said I.

"Oh, nonsense!" said Mrs. Hilary.

But there are — and I did n't go.

XIX

THE OTHER LADY

"BY the merest chance," I observed meditatively, "I attended a reception last night."

"I went to three," said Lady Micklcham, selecting a sardine-sandwich with care.

"I might not have gone," I mused. "I might easily not have gone."

"I can't see what difference it would make if you had n't," said she.

"I thought three times about going. It's a curious world."

"What happened? You may smoke, you know."

"I fell in love," said I, lighting a cigarette.

Lady Mickleham placed her feet on the fender — it was a chilly afternoon — and turned her face to me, shielding it from the fire with her handkerchief.

"Men of your age," she remarked, "have no business to be thinking of such things."

"I was not thinking of it," said I. "I was thinking of going home. Then I was introduced to her."

"And you stayed a little, I suppose?"

"I stayed two hours — or two minutes; I forget which;" and I added, nodding my head at Lady Mickleham, "There was something irresistible about me last night."

Lady Mickleham laughed.

"You seem very pleased with yourself," she said, reaching for a fan to replace the handkerchief.

"Yes, take care of your complexion," said I, approvingly. "She has a lovely complexion."

Lady Mickleham laid down the fan.

"I am very pleased with myself," I continued. "She was delighted with me."

"I suppose you talked nonsense to her."

"I have not the least idea what I talked to her. It was quite immaterial. The language of the eyes —"

"Oh, you might be a boy!"

"I was," said I, nodding again.

There was a long silence. Dolly looked at me; I looked at the fire. I did not, however, see the fire. I saw something quite different.

"She liked me very much," I observed, stretching my hands out towards the blaze.

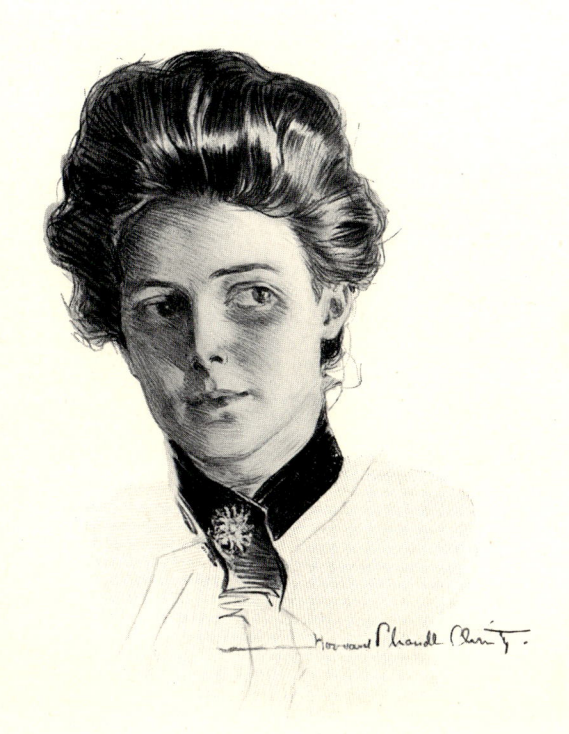

"You seem very pleased with yourself," said Dolly

THE OTHER LADY

"You absurd old man!" said Dolly. "Was she very charming?"

"She was perfect."

"How? Clever?"

I waved my hand impatiently.

"Pretty, Mr. Carter?"

"Why, of course; the prettiest creature I ever — But that goes without saying."

"It would have gone better without saying," remarked Dolly. "Considering — "

To have asked "Considering what?" would have been the acme of bad taste. I merely smiled, and waved my hand again.

"You're quite serious about it, aren't you?" said Dolly.

"I should think I was," said I, indignantly. "Not to be serious in such a matter is to waste it utterly."

"I'll come to the wedding," said Dolly.

"There won't be a wedding," said I. "There are Reasons."

"Oh! You're very unlucky, Mr. Carter."

"That," I observed, "is as it may be, Lady Mickleham."

"Were the Reasons at the reception?"

"They were. It made no difference."

"It's very curious," remarked Dolly, with a compassionate air, "that you always manage to admire people whom somebody else has married."

"It would be very curious," I rejoined, "if somebody had not married the people whom I admire. Last night, though, I made nothing of his sudden removal: my fancy rioted in accidental deaths for him."

"He won't die," said Dolly.

"I hate that sort of superstition," said I, irritably. "He's just as likely to die as any other man is."

"He certainly won't die," said Dolly.

"Well, I know he won't. Do let it alone," said I, much exasperated. It was probably only kindness, but Dolly suddenly turned her eyes away from me and fixed them on the fire; she took the fan up again and twirled it in her hand; a queer little smile bent her lips.

"I hope the poor man won't die," said Dolly, in a low voice.

"If he had died last night!" I cried longingly. Then, with a regretful shrug of my shoulders, I added, "Let him live now to the crack of doom!"

Somehow this restored my good humour. I rose and stood with my back to the fire, stretching myself and sighing luxuriously. Dolly leant back in her chair and laughed at me.

"Do you expect to be forgiven?" she asked.

"No, no," said I; "I had too good an excuse."

THE OTHER LADY

"I wish I'd been there — at the reception, I mean."

"I'm extremely glad you weren't, Lady Mickleham. As it was, I forgot all my troubles."

Dolly is not resentful; she did not mind the implied description. She leant back, smiling still. I sighed again, smiled at Dolly, and took my hat. Then I turned to the mirror over the mantelpiece, arranged my necktie, and gave my hair a touch.

"No one," I observed, "can afford to neglect the niceties of the toilet. Those dainty little curls on the forehead — "

"You've had none there for ten years," cried Lady Mickleham.

"I did not mean my forehead," said I.

Sighing once again, I held out my hand to Dolly.

"Are you doing anything this evening?" she asked.

"That depends on what I'm asked to do," said I, cautiously.

"Well, Archie's going to be at the House, and I thought you might take me to the Phaetons' party. It's quite a long drive — a horribly long drive, Mr. Carter."

I stood for a moment considering this proposal.

"I don't think," said I, "that it would be proper."

"Why, Archie suggested it! You're making an excuse. You know you are!" and Lady Mickleham looked very indignant. "As if," she added scornfully, "you cared about what was proper!"

I dropped into a chair, and said in a confidential tone, "I don't care a pin. It was a mere excuse. I don't want to come."

"You're very rude, indeed. Many women would never speak to you again."

"They would," said I, "all do just as you will."

"And what's that, Mr. Carter?"

"Ask me again on the first opportunity."

"Why won't you come?" said Dolly, waiving this question.

I bent forward, holding my hat in my left hand, and sawing the air with my right forefinger.

"You fail to allow," said I, impressively, "for the rejuvenescence which recent events have produced in me. If I came with you this evening I should be quite capable —" I paused.

"Of anything dreadful?" asked Dolly.

"Of paying you pronounced attentions," said I, gravely.

"That," said Dolly, with equal gravity, "would be very regrettable. It would be unjust to me — and very insulting to her, Mr. Carter."

THE OTHER LADY

"It would be the finest testimonial to her," I cried.

"And you'll spend the evening thinking of her?" asked Dolly.

"I shall get through the evening," said I, "in the best way I can." And I smiled contentedly.

"What's her husband?" asked Dolly, suddenly.

"Her husband," I rejoined, "is nothing at all."

Dolly, receiving this answer, looked at me with a pathetic air.

"It's not quite fair," she observed. "Do you know what I'm thinking about, Mr. Carter?"

"Certainly I do, Lady Mickleham. You are thinking that you would like to meet me for the first time."

"Not at all. I was thinking that it would be amusing if you met me for the first time."

I said nothing. Dolly rose and walked to the window. She swung the tassel of the blind and it bumped against the window. The failing sun caught her ruddy brown hair. There were curls on her forehead, too.

"It's a grand world," said I. "And, after all, one can grow old very gradually."

"You're not really old," said Dolly, with the fleetest glance at me. A glance should not be over-long.

"Gradually and disgracefully," I murmured.

THE DOLLY DIALOGUES

"If you met me for the first time—" said Dolly, swinging the tassel.

"By Heaven, it should be the last!" I cried, and I rose to my feet.

Dolly let the tassel go, and made me a very pretty curtsey.

"I am going to another party to-night," said I, nodding my head significantly.

"Ah!" said Dolly.

"And I shall again," I pursued, "spend my time with the prettiest woman in the room."

"Shall you?" asked Dolly, smiling.

"I am a very fortunate fellow," I observed. "And as for Mrs. Hilary, she may say what she likes."

"Oh, does Mrs. Hilary know the—Other Lady?"

I walked towards the door.

"There is," said I, laying my hand on the door, "no Other Lady."

"I shall get there about eleven," said Dolly.

XX

A LIFE SUBSCRIPTION

"I NEVER quite know," said Mrs. Hilary, taking up her embroidery, "what you mean when you talk about love."

"No more do I," I admitted, stroking the cat.

"If you mean that you dedicate to a woman your whole life —"

"And more than half your income."

Mrs. Hilary laid down the embroidery, and observed, as though she were concluding the discussion, —

"The fact is, you don't know what real love is."

"I never met anyone who did," said I.

Mrs. Hilary opened her mouth.

"At least they could never tell me what it was," I added hastily.

Mrs. Hilary resumed the embroidery.

"Now the other day," I continued, "my friend Major Camperton married his cook."

"What for?" cried Mrs. Hilary.

"Because his wife was dead," said I.

"That's not a reason."

"You must admit that it's an excuse," I pleaded.

Mrs. Hilary, taking no notice of my apology, made a thoughtful stitch or two. Then she observed, —

"I was never in love with any man except Hilary."

"You're always boasting of that: I suppose it was difficult?"

"But once I was awfully — but if I tell you, you'll talk about it."

"Upon my honour I won't."

"You will — to Lady Mickleham."

"Lady Mickleham takes no interest in you," said I.

"Well, once I was awfully tempted. It was before I knew Hilary."

"But after you knew me?" I suggested.

"Don't be absurd," said Mrs. Hilary. "He was very rich — rather handsome too."

"I have always persisted in maintaining that you were human," I observed complacently.

"I think," said she, gazing at me, "that you are the most *earthly* man I ever knew."

"Go on with the story," said I, taking the cat on my knee.

"And he was really very fond of me."

"*Are n't you ever going to marry?*"

A LIFE SUBSCRIPTION

"Oh, so he said."

"But — well, I might have, if he had n't."

"Oh, I understand; at least I hope so."

"I mean he would n't talk about anything else."

"I suppose he saw nothing else in you."

"That was what I felt. Good looks are n't everything."

"Were you good-looking?" I inquired.

Mrs. Hilary showed signs of being about to take up her embroidery.

"All right: Hilary is n't here," said I, in excuse.

"I hated it. I wanted to be — " She paused.

"What's in a word? Say 'esteemed.'"

"Yes — for something more than that."

"So you would n't have anything to say to him?"

"No. I was so glad — afterwards."

"And what's become of him?"

"Oh, he's married."

"It's a just world. Now lots of those immoral writers would have rewarded him with perpetual bachelorhood."

Mrs. Hilary pushed her embroidery quite far off, and leant forward towards me.

"Are n't you *ever* going to marry?" she asked.

"Marriages are made in heaven," said I. Mrs. Hilary nodded approvingly. "I thought of waiting till I got there," I added.

THE DOLLY DIALOGUES

"Oh," said Mrs. Hilary. And she added, "I know a really charming girl."

"You cruel woman! Would you doom her to me?"

"You'd be all right," said Mrs. Hilary, "if you could be removed from —"

"Certain influences," I suggested hastily. "But for Hilary you also would be a pleasant woman."

"There's not the least comparison," said she, with a flush.

"There's always a comparison," I observed. "What are we talking about?"

Now Mrs. Hilary could not, as I well knew, answer this question.

"Well, I'm very sorry about it," she said.

"A romance," said I, "is a thing to be cherished."

"I can't think it's right," said Mrs. Hilary.

"To remember — to be proud of."

"I don't want to be hard about it," murmured Mrs. Hilary.

"To be taken —"

"Seriously? Yes, of course, or it's worse than —"

"To be taken," said I, "between meals."

Mrs. Hilary leapt to her feet.

"Or else you know," I added, "it would spoil dinner."

Mrs. Hilary was very angry; but she was also

A LIFE SUBSCRIPTION

a little curious. The latter emotion was more powerful.

"I wonder," said she, "what you do really feel about —"

"What?"

"It," said Mrs. Hilary.

"Am I in the confessional?"

To my delight a smile lurked round Mrs. Hilary's lips.

"You think," she said, "that I don't understand it. Well, I do a little. She's been here."

"Has she, though? What was she doing here?"

"Oh, coaxing," said Mrs. Hilary. "She wanted a subscription from Hilary."

I was much interested.

"Were you present at the interview?" I asked.

"Yes," said Mrs. Hilary. "She got the subscription, Mr. Carter, — a larger one than Hilary could afford."

"I have given her a larger one than I could afford."

The rare smile still twitched round Mrs. Hilary's mouth.

"What do you think Hilary did when she'd gone?" she asked.

"I should think he felt a fool," said I.

"He apologised," said Mrs. Hilary.

THE DOLLY DIALOGUES

I laughed. Mrs. Hilary laughed reluctantly.

"Guileless creature!" I observed.

"Oh, you need n't do that!" she said, with a slight flush. "Shall I tell you what he did afterwards?"

"Lord, I know that well enough!"

"I 'm sure you don't."

"Gave you a new bonnet, of course."

I believe that Mrs. Hilary was annoyed; for she said quite sulkily,—

"It was a bracelet."

"I told you so," I observed.

"He'd have given it me anyhow," she cried.

"Not he!" said I.

"He 'd meant to, before," said she. "He said so."

I smiled; but I did not wish to make mischief, so I added, "The subscription was, of course, civility."

"That 's all, of course. Still it is funny, is n't it?"

"Perhaps it is rather."

There was a pause.

"Do you care to meet that girl?" asked Mrs. Hilary.

"N-no," said I.

"I would give you one more chance," she said generously.

"*Oh, mine's a life subscription*"

A LIFE SUBSCRIPTION

"Thank you. I'm still subscribing," I answered. "No bracelets for me."

"We laughed about it when she was gone. Hilary was amused at himself."

"I have experienced the feeling," I observed.

"I wonder if I ought to tell you what he called her?"

"Probably not. Go on."

"He said she was an insinuating little —"

"Why do you hesitate, Mrs. Hilary?"

"*Devil*," said Mrs. Hilary, almost under her breath.

"Ah!" said I, setting the cat down, and reaching for my hat.

"Yes, devil," said Mrs. Hilary, more courageously.

"And what did he say you were?" I asked.

"Oh, nothing," said Mrs. Hilary, blushing.

"Then you and Hilary are friends again?"

"I didn't mind in the least," declared Mrs. Hilary. "Only it's curious —"

I began to laugh. I enjoy a chance of laughing at Mrs. Hilary.

"We are all much indebted to her," said I; "some for a bracelet —"

"Nonsense!"

"Some for a momentary emotion —"

"He didn't feel even that."

"Some for a life-long — Dear me, how late it grows! I must be off." And I held out my hand. As I did so, Hilary entered.

"By the way, Carter," said he, when he saw me, "what's that society Lady Mickleham collects for? She got something out of me. I hope it's not a fraud."

"I hope not," said I.

"Because I've given her a trifle."

"So have I," I remarked.

"A donation, you know."

"Oh, mine's a life subscription," said I.

"Oh, go away," said Mrs. Hilary, impatiently.

"Well, you've got nothing else to do with your money," said Hilary. "You've not got a wife and family."

"That is, of course," said I, "the explanation."

Then Mrs. Hilary drove me out. She'd have done it sooner only that in her heart she credits me with a tragedy.

XXI

WHAT MIGHT HAVE BEEN

UNFORTUNATELY it was Sunday; therefore the gardeners could not be ordered to shift the long row of flower-pots from the side of the terrace next the house, where Dolly had ordered them to be put, to the side remote from the house, where Dolly now wished them to stand. Yet Dolly could not think of living with the pots where they were till Monday. It would kill her, she said. So Archie left the cool shade of the great trees, where Dolly sat doing nothing, and Nellie Phaeton sat splicing the gig whip, and I lay in a deck-chair, with something iced beside me. Outside, the sun was broiling hot, and poor Archie mopped his brow at every weary journey across the broad terrace.

"It's a burnin' shame, Dolly," said Miss Phaeton. "I wouldn't do it if I were him."

"Oh, yes, you would, dear," said Dolly. "The pots looked atrocious on that side."

THE DOLLY DIALOGUES

I took a long sip from my glass, and observed in a meditative tone, —

"There, but for the grace of woman, goes Samuel Travers Carter."

Dolly's lazy lids half lifted. Miss Phaeton mumbled (her mouth was full of twine), —

"What *do* you mean?"

"*Nemo omnibus horis sapit*," said I, apologetically.

"I don't know what that means either."

"*Nemo* — everybody," I translated, "*sapit* — has been in love — *omnibus* — once — *horis* — at least."

"Oh, and you mean she would n't have you?" asked Nellie, with blunt directness.

"Not quite that," said I. "They — "

"They?" murmured Dolly, with half-lifted lids.

"*They*," I pursued, "regretfully recognised my impossibility. Hence I am not carrying pots across a broad terrace under a hot sun."

"Why did they think you impossible?" asked Miss Phaeton, who takes much interest in this sort of question.

"A variety of reasons: for one I was too clever, for another too stupid; for others too good — or too bad; too serious — or too frivolous; too poor or — "

"Well, no one objected to your money, I suppose?" interrupted Nellie.

WHAT MIGHT HAVE BEEN

"Pardon me. I was about to say 'or not rich enough.'"

"But that's the same thing."

"The antithesis is certainly imperfect," I admitted.

"Mr. Gay," said Nellie, introducing the name with some timidity, "you know who I mean?— the poet— once said to me that man was essentially imperfect until he was married."

"It is true," I agreed. "And woman until she is dead."

"I don't think he meant it quite in that sense," said Nellie, rather puzzled.

"I don't think he meant it in any sense," murmured Dolly, a little unkindly.

We might have gone on talking in this idle way for ever so long had not Archie at this point dropped a large flower-pot and smashed it to bits. He stood looking at the bits for a moment, and then came towards us and sank into a chair.

"I'm off!" he announced.

"And half are on one side, and half on the other," said Dolly, regretfully.

A sudden impulse seized me. I got up, put on my straw hat, took off my coat, walked out into the sun, and began to move flower-pots across the broad terrace. I heard a laugh from Archie, a little cry from Dolly, and from Nellie Phaeton,

"Goodness! what's he doin' that for?" I was not turned from my purpose. The luncheon bell rang. Miss Phaeton, whip and twine in hand, walked into the house. Archie followed her, saying as he passed that he hoped I should n't find it warm. I went on shifting the flower-pots. They were very heavy. I broke two, but I went on. Presently Dolly put up her parasol and came out from the shade to watch me. She stood there for a moment or two. Then she said, —

"Well, do you think you'd like it, Mr. Carter?"

"Wait till I've finished," said I, waving my hand.

Another ten minutes saw the end of my task. Panting and hot, I sought the shade, and flung myself on to my deck-chair again. I also lit a cigarette.

"I think they looked better on the other side, after all," said Dolly, meditatively.

"Of course you do," said I, urbanely. "You need n't tell me that."

"Perhaps you'd like to move them back," she suggested.

"No," said I. "I've done enough to create the impression."

"And how did you like it?"

"It was," said I, "in its way a pleasant enough

WHAT MIGHT HAVE BEEN

illusion." And I shrugged my shoulders, and blew a ring of smoke.

To my very considerable gratification, Dolly's tone manifested some annoyance as she asked, —

"Why do you say 'in its way'?"

"Because, in spite of the momentary pleasure I gained from feeling myself a married man, I could not banish the idea that we should not permanently suit one another."

"Oh, you thought that?" said Dolly, smiling again.

"I must confess it," said I. "The fault, I know, would be mine."

"I'm sure of that," said Dolly.

"But the fact is that I can't exist in too high altitudes. The rarefaction of the moral atmosphere—"

"Please don't use all those long words."

"Well, then, to put it plainly," said I, with a pleasant smile, "I felt all the time that Mrs. Hilary would be too good for me."

It is not very often that it falls to my humble lot to startle Lady Mickleham out of her composure. But at this point she sat up quite straight in her chair; her cheeks flushed, and her eyelids ceased to droop in indolent *insouciance*.

"Mrs. Hilary!" she said. "What has Mrs. Hilary—?"

THE DOLLY DIALOGUES

"I really thought you understood," said I, "the object of my experiment."

Dolly glanced at me. I believe that my expression was absolutely innocent — and I am, of course, sure that hers expressed mere surprise.

"I thought," she said, after a pause, "that you were thinking of Nellie Phaeton."

"Oh, I see," cried I, smiling. "A natural mistake, to be sure!"

"She thought so too," pursued Dolly, biting her lip.

"Did she, though?"

"And I'm sure she'd be quite annoyed if she thought you were thinking of Mrs. Hilary."

"As a matter of fact," I observed, "she didn't understand what I was doing at all."

Dolly leant back. The relics of a frown still dwelt on her brow; presently, however, she began to swing her hat on her forefinger, and she threw a look at me. I immediately looked up towards the branches above my head.

"We might as well go in to lunch," said Dolly.

"By all means," I acquiesced, with alacrity.

We went out into the sunshine, and came where the pots were. Suddenly Dolly said, —

"Go back and sit down again, Mr. Carter."

"I want my lunch," I ventured to observe.

WHAT MIGHT HAVE BEEN

"Do as I tell you," said Dolly, stamping her foot; whereat, much intimidated, I went back, and stretched myself once more on the deck-chair.

Dolly approached a flower-pot. She stooped down, exerted her strength, lifted it, and carried it, not without effort, across the terrace. Again she did the like. I sat smoking and watching. She lifted a third pot, but dropped it halfway. Then, dusting her hands against one another, she came back slowly into the shade and sat down. I made no remark. Dolly glanced at me.

"Well?" she said.

"Woman — woman — woman!" said I, sadly.

"Must I carry some more?" asked Dolly, in a humble yet protesting tone.

"Mrs. Hilary," I began, "is an exceedingly attractive — "

Dolly rose with a sigh.

"Where are you going?" I asked.

"More pots," said Dolly, standing opposite me. "I must go on, you see."

"Till when, Lady Mickleham?"

"Till you tell the truth," said Dolly, and she suddenly burst into a little laugh.

"Woman — woman — woman!" said I again. "Let's go in to lunch."

"I'm going to carry the pots," said Dolly. "It's awfully hot, Mr. Carter — and look at my poor hands!"

THE DOLLY DIALOGUES

She held them out to me.

"Lunch!" said I.

"Pots!" said Dolly, with infinite firmness.

The window of the dining-room opened and Archie put his head out.

"Come along, you two," he called. "Everything's getting cold."

Dolly turned an appealing glance on me.

"How obstinate you are!" she said. "You know perfectly well—"

I began to walk towards the house.

"I'm going in to lunch," said I.

"Ask them to keep some for me," said Dolly, and she turned up the sleeves of her gown till her wrists were free.

"It's most unfair," said I, indignantly.

"I don't care if it is," said Dolly, stooping down to lift a pot.

I watched her strain to lift it. She had chosen the largest and heaviest; she sighed delicately and delicately she panted. She also looked at her hands, and held them up for me to see the lines of brown on the pink. I put my hands in my pockets and said most sulkily, as I turned away towards the house,—

"All right. It wasn't Mrs. Hilary, then."

Dolly rose up, seized me by the arm, and made me run to the house.

WHAT MIGHT HAVE BEEN

"Mr. Carter," she cried, "would stop for those wretched pots. He's moved all except two, but he's broken three. Is n't he stupid?"

"You are an old ass, Carter," said Archie.

"I believe you 're right, Archie," said I.

XXII

A FATAL OBSTACLE

"WHAT I can't make out," I observed (addressing myself to Lady Jane), "is why women don't fall in love with me. I'm all a man should be, and a reasonable number of things that he should n't."

Lady Jane always tries to be polite.

"Perhaps it's just that you don't find it out," she suggested after a moment's consideration.

"I shall adopt that view," said I, cordially. "It will add a spice to the most formal greeting."

"It'll make you do awfully silly things," remarked Dolly, with an air of experience.

Lady Jane was looking thoughtful. "Mamma says love comes with marriage," she went on presently.

"Yes, generally," I assented. "Not," I added, turning to Dolly, "that three in a brougham is really comfortable, you know."

"One has to invite him sometimes," Dolly murmured.

A FATAL OBSTACLE

"Oh, but I'm sure mamma meant—"

"Mamma meant that you'd been flirting with the curate, Jane."

"Dorothea dear!" gasped Lady Jane.

"The secret of love lies, I suppose, in unselfishness." (I threw out the suggestion in a tentative way.)

"That's what makes Archie such a good husband," said Dolly.

"It must, of course, exist on both sides, Lady Mickleham."

"Oh, no, that's tiresome. It's like getting through the door,—nobody'll go first."

"True. You spend all your time trying to be allowed to do what you don't want to do; and the other party does the same."

"Mr. Shenton says that the power of sympathy is the real secret of it." Mr. Shenton, by the way, is the curate.

I glanced at Dolly and shook my head; she nodded approvingly. Thus buttressed, I remarked deliberately,—

"The power of sympathy has wrecked far more homes than it has—er—blessed. I would, on the whole, back it against the Victoria Cross."

"I think I could love a man just for being good," mused Lady Jane.

"Oh, you impossible kind of an old dear!"

Dolly gurgled affectionately. "Besides, that's no use to poor Mr. Carter."

"I am not so very bad," said I. "Come now, we'll run through my vices and—"

"I think I forgot to water that fern," said Lady Jane, rather suddenly.

"There was once a governess—" I began, thinking to beguile Dolly's leisure with the story. Lady Jane had left us.

"I know about that. Mrs. Hilary told me."

"Then you're quite friends now?"

"Not particularly, but one must talk about something.— There was another girl in love with you once, too."

"Why not have told me at the time? I should have enjoyed it."

"I mustn't tell you her name."

I did not speak for a moment.

"Well, then, it was Agatha Hornton."

"Agatha Martin that is?"

"I suppose she thought that, as you were hopeless" (Dolly was seeming a good deal amused at something), "she might as well marry Captain Martin."

"One can be unhappy without being absurd," said I, rather crossly. "Dear, dear! 'Having known me, to decline—'"

"Decline? I didn't say she absolutely asked you!"

"*She used to bore me awfully about you*"

A FATAL OBSTACLE

"I wish you would read a little poetry sometimes. Your ignorance cramps my conversation. Was she very fond of me?"

"She thought you *handsome*," said Dolly, conclusively.

"It was a *grande passion*?"

"Oh, no. She'd been very well brought up. But she just adored you."

"She was a nice girl,—a thoroughly nice girl. I never thought much of Martin. Ugly fellow, too."

"She used to bore me awfully about you. You see, I was her great friend, and she knew she could trust me."

"Not to give her away?"

"Yes," said Dolly, gently caressing the Japanese pug that the Admiral Commanding on the Pacific Station has recently sent her.

"It's beautiful how you women stand by one another," I observed. "What was it that particularly attracted her in me?"

"I really cannot think," said Dolly; "any more than I can think what attracted — Oh, do you mind ringing the bell? It's Fushahima's tea-time."

"I wish she took it a minute later," said I, as I obeyed. "Martin was a very dull chap, you know."

"Something seems to have set you thinking of Captain Martin."

"I met them all coming back from church (they were coming back, I mean) a Sunday or two ago. Four, are n't there?"

"Five. Three girls and two boys."

"Getting big too, are n't they?"

"Fine children, Mr. Carter," observed Dolly, cheerfully.

"She was certainly a clever girl — in those days."

"Ah, in those days!" Dolly murmured with an indulgent smile, — one that means you can go on if you like, but that you are obviously rather foolish.

"Idyllic happiness," said I, resuming my seat, "comes to very few of us, Lady Mickleham."

"Well, one marries, or something, you see."

"There is, of course, one's career."

"Archie's quite keen on being an Under-Secretary."

"I may not understand, but I am willing to admire. Why did n't the girl encourage me? I expect that's all I wanted."

"Well, what do you mean by encouragement?" asked Dolly, pulling Fushahima's ears; she is always alive to the artistic value of the brute creation.

A FATAL OBSTACLE

"What I mean by it is conveying, however delicately, that I was the only man in the world she ever did or ever could care for. Isn't that what you used to mean by it, Lady Mickleham?"

"You can take Fushahima, Pattern," said Dolly.

"Yes, my lady."

"Not too much cream in her milk."

"Very good, my lady."

"What were you saying, Mr. Carter?"

"I forget, my lady."

There was a moment's silence — sometimes there should be.

Then I took my tea and stood on the hearth-rug, drinking it.

"Solitude, I believe, has its consolations, when one looks at other people's families. Besides, it's surprising the number of little luxuries I get for nothing."

"For nothing?"

"Well, out of Mrs. Carter's dress-allowance. It's quite moderate,— only four hundred a year,— but it keeps a cab, and buys a little drawing, perhaps, and so on. It's a great comfort, I assure you."

Dolly began to laugh gently.

"She'd have exceeded it, and I never do more than anticipate it," I pursued.

"I've sometimes wondered at your extravagance."

"Ah, well, you understand it now."

"Did the allowance include frocks for the girls?"

"Pray curb your imagination, Lady Mickleham."

"You quite shuddered!"

"I had visions of short stiff frocks and long black stockings — like a family group at the Royal Academy — all legs and innocence, you know."

"Yes, and all named Carter!" sighed Dolly, with a commiserating air.

"You don't like the name?"

"Not much."

I looked at Dolly. I think we must have smiled.

"I might have known there was some such reason," said I.

"I do wonder what's become of Jane, and why they don't bring Fushahima back," said Dolly.

"It's always a comfort to get at the real reason of anything. Now if my name had been Vavasour — or — "

"I don't mind 'Mr. Carter' so much, but 'Mrs. Carter' sounds horrible," Dolly explained.

"Girls being, as we all know, in the habit of writing the competing names in conjunction with

A FATAL OBSTACLE

their own Christian names on the backs of envelopes and the fly-leaves of library books, in order to see how they look, I can well understand that if it came to a choice between Carter and — "

At this point, before I had fully developed my remark, Lady Jane came back. She sometimes does by accident what the Dowager would do on purpose. Heredity, I imagine.

"I've been thinking about it," said Lady Jane, "and I'm quite sure it's goodness of heart."

"A fatal obstacle!" I said, shaking my head despondently.

"Another!" murmured Dolly, with a lift of her brows.

"Shining through, you know, Mr. Carter," added Lady Jane.

"I really don't see the use of continuing the conversation."

"You must encourage him, Dorothea," said Lady Jane, with a smile.

Dolly laughed; I won't swear she didn't blush just a trifle.

"Oh, I've given up trying to do that long ago, Jane dear," said she.

"She used to succeed far too well, you know. Oh, but pray allow me to hand you a cup of tea."

I went away soon afterwards. I had to pay a call — on the Martins.

XXIII

THE CURATE'S BUMP

"WHAT is the harm?" I asked at lunch, "in being fat?" and I looked round the table.

I had led up to this subject because something which fell from Mrs. Hilary Musgrave the other day led me to suppose that I might appear to be growing stouter than I used to be.

"It doesn't matter in a man," said Nellie Phaeton.

"That," I observed, "is merely part of the favourite pretence of your sex."

"And what's that, Mr. Carter?" asked Dolly.

"That you're indifferent to a pleasing appearance in man. It won't go down."

"It would if you ate less," said Dolly, wilfully misunderstanding me.

"Napoleon was fat," remarked Archie; he is studying history.

"Mamma is rather fat," said Lady Jane, breaking a long silence; her tone seemed to imply that it was a graceful concession on the Dowager's part.

THE CURATE'S BUMP

"I shouldn't say you ever had much of a figure," observed Dolly, gazing at me dispassionately.

"Mamma," resumed Lady Jane, with an amiable desire to give me useful information, "drinks nothing but lemonade. I make it hot for her and—"

"I should like to do that," said I, longingly.

"It's the simplest thing in the world," cried Lady Jane. "You can do it for yourself. You just take—"

"A pretty girl," I murmured absently. "I—I beg your pardon, Lady Jane. You see, Miss Phaeton is opposite and my thoughts wandered."

"It's no use talkin' sensibly where you are," said Miss Nellie, very severely, and she rose from the table.

"Won't anyone have any rice pudding?" asked Archie, appealingly.

"If I were a camel I would," said I.

"Why a camel, Mr. Carter?" asked Lady Jane.

"A camel, Lady Jane, is so constructed that it could keep one exclusively for rice pudding."

"One what, Mr. Carter?"

I strolled to the window, where Dolly stood looking out.

"Dear Jane!" said Dolly. "She never sees anything."

"I wish there were more like her," said I, cordially. "She does n't inherit it from her mother, though."

"No, the Dowager sees a great deal more than there is there," laughed Dolly, glancing at me.

"But fortunately," said I, "not all there is in other places."

"Mamma says—" we heard Lady Jane remarking at the table. We strolled out into the garden.

"Now, is n't that provoking?" cried Dolly. "They have n't rolled the tennis lawn, and the people will be here directly."

"Shall I ask Archie to ask somebody to get somebody?"

"They 've all gone to dinner, I expect. Suppose you roll it, Mr. Carter. It 'll be so good for you. Exercise is what you want."

"Exercise is, no doubt, what I need," said I, doubtfully eying the roller.

"It 's the same thing," said Dolly.

"It 's an Eternal Antithesis," said I, taking off my coat.

I began to roll. Dolly stood watching me for a moment. Then she went indoors. I went on rolling. Presently, raising my eyes from my task, I found the curate looking on; he was in flannels and carried a racket.

"*Now, isn't that provoking?*" *cried Dolly.*
"*They haven't rolled the tennis lawn*"

THE CURATE'S BUMP

"Although," I observed to the curate, "I have convinced my reason that there is no harm in being fat, yet, sooner than be fat, I roll. Can you explain that?"

"Reason is not everything," said the curate.

"Your cloth obliges you to that," said I, suspiciously.

"I'm in flannels to-day," enjoined the curate, with a smile.

I liked that. I loosed my hold of the roller and took the curate's arm. We began to walk up and down.

"There is also," said I, "romance!"

"There's little enough of that for most of us," said the curate.

"There has been too much for some of us," I returned. "But the lawn is smooth where the roller has been. The bumps — the pleasant bumps — are gone."

"They spoilt the game," observed the curate.

"They made the game," said I, frowning a little.

There was silence for a minute. Then the curate asked, —

"Is Lady Jane going to play to-day?"

"I seemed like Fate with that roller," said I. "Or like Time."

The curate smiled absently.

"Or like Morality," I pursued.

The curate smiled indulgently; he was in flannels, good man.

"As to Lady Jane," said I, recollecting myself, "I don't know."

"It's of no consequence," murmured the curate.

At once I knew that it was of consequence — to the curate. But my thoughts drifted in another direction, and, when I emerged from the reverie, I saw Lady Jane and the curate strolling together on the lawn, and Lady Mickleham approaching me in a white gown; she carried a red parasol.

"Archie and Nellie will be out directly," said she, "and then you can begin."

"They can," said I, putting on my coat and lighting a cigarette.

"Look at that poor dear man with Jane!" exclaimed Dolly. "Now should you have thought that Jane was the sort of person to — ?"

"Everybody," said I, "is the sort of person — if the other person is."

"Of course he knows it's hopeless. The Dowager would n't hear of it."

"Really? And she hears of so many things!"

Dolly, after a contemptuous glance, began to inspect the lawn. I retired into the shade and sat down. Lady Jane and the curate strolled a little

THE CURATE'S BUMP

further off. Presently I was roused by an accusing cry from Dolly.

"She's found a bump," said I to myself, shaking my head.

"You can never do things properly," said Dolly, walking up to me.

"I certainly can't do many things in the way I should prefer," I admitted.

"You've left a great bump in the middle of the Court."

My eyes strayed from Dolly to Lady Jane and the curate, and thence back to Dolly.

"It's not my bump," said I; "it's the curate's."

"You're getting into the habit," remarked Dolly, "of being unintelligible. I'm sure there's nothing clever in it. I met a man the other day who said he never understood what you meant."

"You'd understand if you'd stayed; why did you go away?"

"To change," answered Dolly.

I was pleased.

"It's an old trick of yours," said I.

"What did you mean by the bump being the curate's?" asked Dolly, returning to the point.

I entered into an explanation. There was plenty of time; the curate and Lady Jane were strolling, the click of billiard balls through the open windows accounted for Nellie and Archie.

"I see," said Dolly. "Poor man! Do you think he'd like it left?"

I walked leisurely towards the roller, Dolly following me.

"If it were my bump," said I, laying hold of the roller, and looking at Lady Mickleham.

Lady Mickleham smiled — under protest. It is a good enough variety of smile.

"If it were my bump," said I, "I should reduce it — so — and so again," and twice I passed the roller gently over the bump.

"It's awfully small now," said Dolly; and her voice sounded regretful.

"It's not so large as it was," said I, cheerfully.

Dolly let down her parasol with a jerk.

"You're horribly disagreeable to-day," she said.

I leant on the handle of the roller and smiled.

"You're very rude and — and — "

"Nobody," said I, "likes to be told that he has no figure."

"You are an Apollo, Mr. Carter," said Dolly.

That was handsome enough.

"I would let it alone, if it were my bump," said I. "Hang these rollers!"

"It is your bump," said Dolly.

As she spoke Archie came out of the billiard room. Lady Jane and the curate hastened to join us. Archie inspected the lawn.

"*You are an Apollo, Mr. Carter*"

THE CURATE'S BUMP

"Why, it's been rolled!" he cried.

"I rolled it," said I, proudly.

"Jove!" said Archie. "Hullo, though, old chap, you haven't been over here."

He had found the bump.

"I have been over there," said I, "oftener than anywhere else."

"Give me the — "

"Now, Archie, do begin to play," said Dolly, suddenly.

"Oh, well, one doesn't hurt," said Archie.

"It won't hurt much," said the curate; upon which I smiled at Lady Jane.

"What is it, Mr. Carter?" she asked.

"He's so right, you know," said I.

XXIV

ONE WAY IN

I HAD a very curious dream the other night. In fact, I dreamt that I was dead. I passed through a green baize door and found myself in a small square room. Opposite me was another door, inscribed "Elysian Fields," and in front of it, at a large table with a raised ledge, sat Rhadamanthus. As I entered, I saw a graceful figure vanish through the door opposite.

"It's no use trying to deceive me," I observed. "That was Mrs. Hilary, I think; if you don't mind, I'll join her."

"I'm afraid I must trouble you to take a seat for a few moments, Mr. Carter," said Rhadamanthus, "while I run over your little account."

"Any formalities which are usual," I murmured politely, as I sat down.

Rhadamanthus turned over the leaves of a large book.

"Carter — Samuel Travers, isn't it?" he asked.

ONE WAY IN

"Yes. For goodness' sake don't confuse me with Vincent Carter. He only paid five shillings in the pound."

"Your case presents some peculiar features, Mr. Carter," said Rhadamanthus. "I hope I am not censorious, but—well, that fine at Bow-street?"

"I was a mere boy," said I, with some warmth, "and my solicitor grossly mismanaged the case."

"Well, well!" said he, soothingly. "But have n't you spent a great deal of time at Monte Carlo?"

"A man must be somewhere," said I.

Rhadamanthus scratched his nose.

"I should have wasted the money anyhow," I added.

"I suppose you would," he conceded. "But what of this *caveat* lodged by the Dowager Lady Mickleham? That's rather serious, you know; is n't it now — joking apart?"

"I am disappointed," I remarked, "to find a man of your experience paying any attention to such an ill-natured old woman."

"We have our rules," he replied, "and I'm afraid, Mr. Carter, that until that *caveat* is removed—"

"You don't mean that?"

"Really, I'm afraid so."

"Then I may as well go back," said I, taking my hat.

At this moment there was a knock at the door.

"Although I can't oblige you with an order of admission," said Rhadamanthus, very civilly, "perhaps it would amuse you to listen to a case or two. There's no hurry, you know. You've got lots of time before you."

"It will be an extremely interesting experience," said I, sitting down again.

The door opened, and, as I expected (I don't know why, but it happens like that in dreams), Dolly Mickleham came in. She did not seem to see me. She bowed to Rhadamanthus, smiled, and took a chair immediately opposite the table.

"Mickleham — Dorothea — Countess of —" she said.

"Formerly, I think, Dolly Foster?" asked Rhadamanthus.

"I don't see what that's got to do with it," said Dolly.

"The account runs on," he explained, and began to consult his big book. Dolly leant back in her chair, slowly peeling off her gloves. Rhadamanthus shut the book with a bang.

"It's not the least use," he said decisively. "It wouldn't be kind to pretend that it was, Lady Mickleham."

ONE WAY IN

"Dear, dear!" said Dolly. "What's the matter?"

"Half the women in London have petitioned against you."

"Have they really?" cried Dolly, to all appearance rather delighted. "What do they say, Mr. Rhadamanthus? Is it in that book? Let me look." And she held out her hand.

"The book's too heavy for you to hold," said he.

"I'll come round," said Dolly. So she went round and leant over his shoulder and read the book.

"What's that scent you've got on?" asked Rhadamanthus.

"Bouquet du diable," said she. (I had never heard of the perfume before.) "Isn't it sweet?"

"I haven't smelt it since I was a boy," sighed Rhadamanthus.

"Poor old thing!" said Dolly. "I'm not going to read all this, you know." And, with a somewhat contemptuous smile, she walked back to her chair. "They ought to be ashamed of themselves," she added, as she sat down. "It's just because I'm not a fright."

"Aren't you a fright?" asked Rhadamanthus. "Where are my spectacles?"

He put them on and looked at Dolly.

"I must go in, you know," said Dolly, smiling at Rhadamanthus. "My husband has gone in!"

"I should n't have thought you 'd consider that conclusive," said he, with a touch of satire in his tone.

"Don't be horrid," said Dolly, pouting.

There was a pause. Rhadamanthus examined Dolly through his spectacles.

"This is a very painful duty," said he, at last. "I have sat here for a great many years, and I have seldom had a more painful duty."

"It's very absurd of you," said Dolly.

"I can't help it, though," said he.

"Do you really mean that I'm not to go in?"

"I do, indeed," said Rhadamanthus.

Dolly rose. She leant her arms on the raised ledge which ran along the table, and she leant her chin on her hands.

"Really?" she said.

"Really," said he, looking the other way.

A sudden change came over Dolly's face. Her dimples vanished: her eyes grew pathetic and began to shine rather than to sparkle: her lip quivered just a little.

"You 're very unkind," she said in an extremely low tone. "I had no idea you would be so unkind."

Rhadamanthus seemed very uncomfortable.

ONE WAY IN

"Don't do that," he said quite sharply, fidgeting with the blotting-paper.

Dolly began to move slowly round the table. Rhadamanthus sat still. When she was standing close by him, she put her hand lightly on his arm and said, —

"Please do, Mr. Rhadamanthus."

"It's as much as my place is worth," he grumbled.

Dolly's eyes shone still, but the faintest little smile began to play about her mouth.

"Some day," she said (with total inappropriateness, now I come to think of it, though it did not strike me so at the time), "you'll be glad to remember having done a kind thing. When you're old — because you are not really old now — you will say, 'I'm glad I didn't send poor Dolly Mickleham away crying.'"

Rhadamanthus uttered an inarticulate sound, — half impatience, half, I fancy, something else.

"We are none of us perfect, I dare say. If I asked your wife — "

"I haven't got a wife," said Rhadamanthus.

"That's why you're so hard-hearted," said Dolly. "A man who's got a wife is never hard on other women."

There was another pause. Then Rhadamanthus, looking straight at the blotting-paper, said, —

"Oh, well, don't bother me. Be off with you;" and as he spoke, the door behind him opened.

Dolly's face broke out into sudden sunshine. Her eyes danced, her dimples capered over her chin.

"Oh, you old dear!" she cried; and, stooping swiftly, she kissed Rhadamanthus. "You're horribly bristly!" she laughed; and then, before he could move, she ran through the door.

I rose from my seat, taking my hat and stick in my hand. I felt, as you may suppose, that I had been there long enough. When I moved, Rhadamanthus looked up, and with an attempt at unconsciousness observed, —

"We will proceed with your case now, if you please, Mr. Carter."

I looked him full in the face. Rhadamanthus blushed. I pursued my way towards the door.

"Stop!" he said, in a blustering tone. "You can't go there, you know."

I smiled significantly.

"Isn't it rather too late for that sort of thing?" I asked. "You seem to forget that I have been here for the last quarter of an hour."

"I didn't know she was going to do it," he protested.

ONE WAY IN

"Oh, of course," said I, "that will be your story. Mine, however, I shall tell in my own way."

Rhadamanthus blushed again. Evidently he felt that he was in a delicate position. We were standing thus, facing one another, when the door began to open again, and Dolly put her head out.

"Oh, it's you, is it?" she said. "I thought I heard your voice. Come along and help me to find Archie."

"This gentleman says I'm not to come in," said I.

"Oh, what nonsense! Now, you really mustn't be silly, Mr. Rhadamanthus — or I shall have to — Mr. Carter, you weren't there, were you?"

"I was — and a more interesting piece of scandal it has seldom been — "

"Hush! I didn't do anything. Now, you know I didn't, Mr. Carter!"

"No," said I, "you didn't. But Rhadamanthus, taking you unawares — "

"Oh, be off with you — both of you!" cried Rhadamanthus.

"That's sensible," said Dolly. "Because, you know, there really isn't any harm in poor Mr. Carter."

Rhadamanthus vanished. Dolly and I went inside.

THE DOLLY DIALOGUES

"I suppose everything will be very different here," said Dolly, and I think she sighed.

Whether it were or not I don't know, for just then I awoke, and found myself saying aloud, in answer to the dream-voice and the dream-face (which had not gone altogether with the dream),

"Not everything,"—a speech that, I agree, I ought not to have made, even though it were only in a dream.